Stacey's Mistake

ANN M. MARTIN

SCHOLASTIC INC.

*This book is in
honor of the birth of my new godson,
Andrew Cleveland Gordon.*

Copyright © 1988 by Ann M. Martin

This book was originally published in paperback by Scholastic Inc. in 1988.

All rights reserved. Published by Scholastic Inc., *Publishers since 1920.* SCHOLASTIC, THE BABY-SITTERS CLUB, and associated logos are trademarks and/or registered trademarks of Scholastic Inc.

The publisher does not have any control over and does not assume any responsibility for author or third-party websites or their content.

No part of this publication may be reproduced, stored in a retrieval system, or transmitted in any form or by any means, electronic, mechanical, photocopying, recording, or otherwise, without written permission of the publisher. For information regarding permission, write to Scholastic Inc., Attention: Permissions Department, 557 Broadway, New York, NY 10012.

ISBN 978-1-338-75553-4

10 9 8 7 6 5 4 3   22 23 24 25

Printed in the U.S.A. 40
This edition first printing 2021

Book design by Maeve Norton

Stacey's Mistake

CHAPTER 1

Dear Stacey,

Hi! I am so, so exited! I cannot wait to see you I realy didn't beleve that the frist time we got to see each other again woud be in new York. Just five more days and we'll be their. I am bringing lots of speding money. Can we go to ~~bloom bloms~~ that big huge depratment store. And lets go to some art musims or at least one. I can't wait!

Luv ya!

Claudia

It could only happen in New York. Only in New York could you be sitting in the middle of your absolutely gorgeous blue-and-white bedroom reading a postcard, and see a gigantic roach sneak out from behind the dresser and have the nerve to run right across the rug and disappear under the closet door. In any other place, a roach would have the good sense to stick to yucky places like laundry rooms or greasy kitchens. But in New York, they get all bold and start invading bedrooms.

My first thought, after he disappeared into the closet was, Oh, disgust. Now do I have to go *look* for him? My second thought was, I sure hope my friends don't see him (or any of his buddies) when they visit this weekend. My friends live in Connecticut, and the worst insect they've ever seen is a bee. A roach would freak them out. (I left the roach alone in the closet. No way was I going after him.)

If I'd known what was going to happen when my friends came, I might have taken the roach as a bad sign, a sign that the weekend was going to be a mistake. (Do you have *any* idea what I'm talking about? You must be pretty confused by now, so I better give you the background to this story.)

For starters, I am Stacey McGill. I'm thirteen years old and I live in New York City. I've lived here all my life, except for last year. Last year, my parents and I moved to Stoneybrook, Connecticut, which was where I met these friends I've been talking about. My friends are Claudia Kishi (she's the one who wrote the postcard), Kristy Thomas, Mary Anne Spier, and Dawn Schafer. The five of us had this neat business called the Baby-sitters Club. But after only a year (well, a year and a couple of months) in Stoneybrook, my mom and dad and I moved back to New York. (These moves have to do with Dad's job, and the explanations for them aren't too interesting.)

I have to admit that I wasn't very upset at the idea of moving back to New York. I've always loved the city, and I missed it when we were in Connecticut. Believe me, I *really* minded the idea of leaving my new friends, but I was thrilled to be getting back to such a bustling, busy place. I love people and stores and shopping and museums and restaurants and theaters. I don't love roaches, but I'll take one or two of them any day over the quiet of Stoneybrook. Stoneybrook is a very pretty little place with nice people, but if you want excitement, you have to drive all the way to Washington Mall, outside of Stamford, which just does not live up to Fifth Avenue.

Anyway, I had moved back to New York, and my friends and I hadn't seen each other in a while.

Claudia and I had just been starting to talk about my visiting Stoneybrook for a weekend, when something happened.

It started with Judy.

I don't know Judy's last name. She's the homeless woman who lives on our block. Now I bet you're wondering about something. You've heard me mention a roach in my bedroom and a homeless woman on my block. Just where in New York do I live? you're probably asking yourself. Well, I live in a very nice neighborhood on the Upper West Side — and so do homeless people. Homelessness is a serious problem in New York. There are thousands and thousands of people like Judy. Some of them live in shelters, some live in subway stations or railroad stations, and some actually live on the street. Judy is one of the ones who actually live on the street. She sleeps in doorways or on top of grates where warm air blows up from the subway. She gets her food from garbage cans or begs for handouts.

It is not a nice life.

I see Judy at least twice a day (when I go back and forth between my nice, comfortable, doorman apartment building and my nice, comfortable private school). Even though I see Judy all the time,

I don't really know what her life is like. I'm sure you can't completely understand homelessness until you've experienced it.

What I see when I see Judy is a woman who looks a lot older than she really is. I see a woman who owns so few things that she won't part with any of them. And I mean, she hangs onto empty tin cans, bottle caps, newspapers, and used plastic cups. She carries her stuff around in old, wrinkled, falling-apart shopping bags. I see a woman who is almost always hungry, who has huge sores on her legs, whose hair is matted, and whose face and hands are permanently red from being exposed to the sun, wind, heat, and cold.

Judy and I couldn't be more different. Yet we're friends. Well, sort of. When Judy is in a good mood, we smile and say hello to each other. Judy calls me Missy. When she's not in a good mood, Judy will stand on the sidewalk and just shout stuff for hours. She screams and yells, then finally she quiets down and mumbles crossly. When she's in those moods, she doesn't call me Missy. She doesn't call me anything. I don't think she even recognizes me.

So what does Judy have to do with my friends'

visit to New York? Well, it's like this: The people on our block who see and hear Judy everyday began to get worried about her. They decided that it was time for them to see what they could do to help Judy and other homeless people in the neighborhood. So they organized a big meeting that was to be held for an entire Saturday afternoon. Most of the adults in my building (including Mom and Dad) were eager to go. Which meant that a lot of kids were going to need baby-sitters. Remember the Baby-sitters Club I belonged to in Stoneybrook? Well, I sort of carried the club back to New York with me, except that I'm the only member of the city branch. For some reason, most of my friends here don't seem interested in sitting. On the one hand, this is nice, because there are plenty of little kids in my building, so I get lots of jobs. On the other hand, I have to turn down lots of jobs, too, and I always feel bad about that. Besides, I miss the meetings our club used to hold.

Well, anyway, a total of five parents called up a whole month in advance to ask me to baby-sit on the afternoon of the big meeting. I felt bad about turning four of the families down, especially when the parents were all going to be at the same place for the same time. If only —

And that was when I got my brilliant idea.

"Mom! Mom!" I called.

I ran into our kitchen. As New York apartments go, ours is fairly large. The clue that you have a large apartment is if you can actually eat in your kitchen. If you've got room for a table and chairs in there, it's a big apartment. And our kitchen had room for a table and chairs.

That was where I found my mom — seated at the table. She was paying bills. I wasn't sure if bill-paying time was the right moment to approach her with my idea, but I decided to risk it.

"What is it, honey?" Mom replied.

I sat down across from her. I explained the baby-sitting situation. Then I said carefully, "Um, remember when Kristy's mother got remarried?"

"Yes?" Mom looked a little confused.

"Remember how the Baby-sitters Club took care of those fourteen children all week before the wedding?"

"Yes?"

"Well, I was thinking. All in all, there are ten kids in the five families that asked me to sit. If my friends were here, we could easily take care of the kids for just one afternoon. And I'm dying to have Claudia and everyone come visit. They could stay for the weekend. What do you think?"

"Four guests?" said Mom thoughtfully. "That seems like a lot of people. It would be fine if it were just Claudia, but —"

"Please?"

"Do you think you're up to it?" asked Mom.

"Of course! I haven't been sick in ages." (I have diabetes, and Mom and Dad worry about me a lot, but lately, as long as I stick to my diet and give myself the insulin injections, I've been just fine.)

"Well," said Mom, "it's okay with me, but you'll need your father's permission, too."

"Thanks, Mom!" I cried. I gave her a kiss. Then I waited for Dad to come home from work. I pounced on him the second he stepped through the door.

"Please, please, please?" I said after I'd explained everything.

Dad adjusted his glasses. At long last he said, "All right."

My parents didn't seem too excited then, but you should have seen them a few days later. They told me I could take Friday off from school that weekend. This was because it turned out that my friends had that Friday off since there was a teachers' convention in Connecticut, so they had a three-day weekend. Mom and Dad said that as long as they were coming into the city — their first trip to New York without their parents along (and Dawn's first trip ever) — they might as well get the most out of it.

Then my parents even suggested that I give a party on Friday night so that my Connecticut friends could meet my New York friends. I couldn't believe my good luck. What a weekend the five of us would have — three days in the city, a party, and a baby-sitting adventure.

Claudia and I called and wrote constantly as the weekend approached.

"What should I wear in New York?" Claud asked once.

"What you wear in Connecticut," I told her.

"Exactly?"

"Believe me, you see *every*thing in the city. Once I saw someone dressed as Batman."

"Maybe it *was* Batman," said Claudia, giggling. "But really. What will your friends wear to the party?"

We weren't getting anywhere. "Wear your black outfit. That really cool one," I told her. Claudia has incredible clothes. And I wanted her to wear this outfit that was sleek and black and covered with silver stars and sparkles.

"Oh, okay," said Claud. "Boy, I am so excited! I don't think I can wait two more weeks. How can I wait two weeks?"

I didn't know. I was dying of excitement myself.

But the two weeks passed — somehow — and finally it was Friday morning, and time for me to get in a cab and meet my friends at Grand Central Station.

CHAPTER 2

Dear Stacey,

I can't wait! I can't wait! I can't wait! New York, here I come! I've been reading everything I can find about New York. Please can we eat at Serendipity, or maybe at the Hard Rock Café, if we can get in there? Do you think we'll see anyone famous? Does anyone famous live in your apartment building? Is your building on the route of the Macy's Thanksgiving Day parade? Just curious.

See you soon!
Love,
Mary Anne

Obviously, Claudia and I weren't the only ones excited about my friends' trip to New York. Mary Anne was nearly frantic. The thing about Mary Anne and New York is that, if this is possible, she has a crush on the city. I'm serious. She's starstruck. She feels the same way about New York that most kids feel about their favorite movie star or rock group. And coming to New York at thirteen without her dad (she'd been here before, but it's different when your father's dragging you around) was for Mary Anne like getting the opportunity to *meet* her idol.

I thought about that as I put my coat on and left our apartment that Friday morning.

"Bye, Mom!" I called.

"Bye, honey! Say hi to everyone for me."

And have fun and be careful, I thought.

"And have fun and be careful!" she added.

It never fails. Mom *always* says that as I leave the apartment. Sometimes I try to escape before the words leave her lips, but so far, I haven't been able to.

In the hallway, I punched the DOWN button and waited for the elevator to arrive. Then came the stomach-tossing ride to the lobby. Our elevator doesn't just rise and fall, it zooms.

The doors opened and I crossed the lobby, calling hello to Lloyd and Isaac, who were on duty at the desk, and thanking James, who held the door open for me. Some people think I'm spoiled, living in this doorman building, but I'll tell you something, I just feel safe. I like doormen for security. (But it *is* nice to have someone hold the door open for you when your hands are full.)

I left our building and walked up the block to Central Park West, where I hailed a cab. Mom gives me cab fare any time I'm going more than ten feet away from the apartment, unless I'm going to be with a group of people. She doesn't like me walking around the city alone, or even taking the bus or subway alone. I can't tell if she's being overprotective or just sensible. In a big city like New York, you really can't be too careful.

I closed the door of the cab. "Grand Central Station, please," I told the driver.

He didn't say anything. (Cabbies hardly ever do.) He just pulled the taxi into the traffic.

I settled back in the seat and thought about the friends I would see soon. In a way, it's surprising that the five of us are friends, because we're so different. Or maybe that's *why* we're friends. Isn't there some old saying about variety being the spice of life? And opposites attracting? If we were alike, we'd probably be really boring and not at all interested in each other. Well, there isn't any danger of that. Let me tell you a little about the friends I was going to meet. I'll start with Kristy Thomas, since she's the president of the club.

If I thought the last year of my life (moving from New York to Connecticut and back again) had been wild, wait till you hear about Kristy's. Kristy, Claudia, and Mary Anne used to live in the same neighborhood. Kristy's house was next door to Mary Anne's (the two of them are best friends), and across the street from Claudia's. At the beginning of seventh grade (last year), Kristy had this idea for starting a baby-sitting service in her neighborhood. She saw how long it sometimes took her mother to find a sitter for David Michael, Kristy's little brother. If Kristy and her big brothers weren't available, her mom sometimes had to make four or five calls before she found someone who was free. So Kristy teamed up with Claudia, Mary Anne, and me, and we formed the Baby-sitters Club. (Dawn joined us later.) We'd meet three times a week, and parents would call us while we were meeting. The great thing about this arrangement was that parents could reach four sitters with just one call, so they were practically guaranteed a sitter. No more calling everyone in the world.

This was Kristy's idea, and it was brilliant. That's one thing Kristy is known for — her brilliant ideas. She has them all the time. The other thing she's known for is her mouth. She can't keep it closed and sometimes it gets her in trouble. I really hoped Kristy would behave herself in New York and not do or say anything embarrassing. But I couldn't count on that. Kristy is a little immature. She even *looks* immature. She's sort of small for her age, and she doesn't pay much attention to her clothes. In fact, she almost always wears the same kind of outfit: jeans, turtleneck, sweater, and running shoes.

What about Kristy's wild year? Well, ever since she was little, Kristy had lived with her two older brothers, Sam and Charlie, David Michael, who's seven now, and her mom, who was divorced. But when Mrs. Thomas decided to marry Watson Brewer, this millionaire she'd been dating, Watson moved Mrs. Thomas and her family across town to his mansion. There, Kristy not only lives in the lap of luxury, but she inherited a stepsister and stepbrother whom she adores, and of course, Watson, her stepfather. What a change for her! (I'm making it sound better than it is. Kristy is still getting used to having been uprooted, and to her new home and neighbors and neighborhood.)

Claudia Kishi is the club's vice president. She's also my best friend. Well, she's my Connecticut best friend. I have a New York best friend, too — Laine Cummings. She'll be at the party tonight, and she and Claudia will meet for the first time. Claudia is the vice president because the girls always hold their meetings in her bedroom. They chose her room because she has a private phone and a private phone number. During meetings, when lots of job calls come in, the girls don't tie up any line but Claudia's. This is important.

I know I said that all the girls in the club are different, but there *are* some similarities between Claudia and me. The two main ones are our taste and the fact that we are (face it) sort of sophisticated. At least, we're more sophisticated than Kristy, Mary Anne, and Dawn are. We both love clothes and wear trendy outfits like short skirts and baggy sweaters. And we both like to do things with our hair. I've been growing mine out a little, so it's just thick and fluffy and blonde. You should see Claud's hair, though. She's Japanese-American and has this long, silky black hair. And boy, does she go out of her way to do special things to it. For instance, she'll part it down the middle, fix one side in three or four braids, and let the other side fall loosely over her shoulder. Also, she's always experimenting with barrettes and hair clips and bows and headbands. Jewelry, too. To top things off, Claudia is just plain gorgeous, with these dark eyes and this creamlike complexion. She has never once had a pimple, and probably never will. Claud's hobbies are art (she's really talented), and reading mysteries. Unfortunately, she's a terrible student, as you could probably tell from her postcard.

The secretary of the Baby-sitters Club is Mary Anne Spier, and she has a big job. She's the one who has to keep the club record book up to date. Kristy insists that the club members, in order to run the business professionally, write a summary of every job they go on. The summaries are recorded in the club notebook. Mary Anne also has to keep up the record book. The most important pages in the record book make up the appointment calendar. There, Mary Anne schedules the sitting jobs. She is careful and neat and rarely makes a mistake.

Although they're best friends, Mary Anne and Kristy are very different. They may both be fairly small for their age (and they even look alike with their brown hair and brown eyes), but the similarities end there. Kristy is loud and sort of cynical; Mary Anne is quiet and shy, dreamy and sensitive (she cries easily). She may even be a little romantic. She's the only one of us to have a steady boyfriend. (His name is Logan Bruno.) And her family is certainly different from Kristy's. While Kristy's was big even before Mrs. Thomas married Watson Brewer, Mary Anne has just her dad and her kitten, Tigger. Mrs. Spier died when Mary Anne was really young. Mr. Spier used to be incredibly strict with Mary Anne, but over the past year, he's loosened up a lot. Now Mary Anne has stopped wearing the jumpers and kilts and loafers her father used to choose for her, and has started wearing more trendy clothes. She's branched out in terms of friends, too. She and Dawn are very close, and then there's Logan. Mary Anne would *never* have had a boyfriend last year . . . .

The other person coming to New York was Dawn Schafer. Dawn is now the treasurer, which used to be my job. Dawn had been a sort of substitute officer (we called her an alternate officer) before I moved, so she easily filled my position. (In case you're wondering, when I left the club, the girls replaced me with two sixth-graders, junior officers named Mallory Pike and Jessi Ramsey. They weren't coming to visit because I didn't know Mal that well and I didn't know Jessi at all. Plus, their parents wouldn't have let them come.) The treasurer's job is to keep track of the money the club members earn, and to collect weekly dues, which are spent on club supplies and stuff.

Dawn was not an original member of the club. She moved to Connecticut from California about four months after Kristy started the club. She moved because her parents got a divorce, so this past year has been a wild one for Dawn, too. Besides having to adjust to life without her father, she had to get used to the East Coast, especially to cold weather. She had to start at a new school in the middle of a year, and make new friends, and her mom had to find a job. Then, not long ago, Dawn's younger brother decided he just couldn't handle that new life, and he moved back to California and Mr. Schafer. Dawn misses her brother a lot, but she seems happy enough. She's very close to her mother. Besides — she's got the Baby-sitters Club!

Dawn is a real individual. She's a health-food

freak. She does things her own way and doesn't care what people think of her. I guess that means she has a lot of self-confidence. And she sure stands out in a crowd. Her hair falls all the way to her waist and is so blonde it's almost white. Her eyes are a clear, pale blue. I remember feeling practically speechless the first time I saw her.

The more I thought about my friends, the more eager I became to see them. But the taxi was just crawling along. We seemed to be approaching a traffic jam at Columbus Circle. There was nothing to do but settle back and wait.

So I did. When we *finally* reached Grand Central, I paid the cabbie and scrambled out of the taxi.

In a few minutes, the members of the Baby-sitters Club would be reunited!

CHAPTER 3

Dear Karen and Andrew,

Hi, you guys! How was your weekend? Did you have fun with your mom? I'm on the train to New York with my friends. What a time we're having. There's a car on the train where you can get snacks and sodas and stuff. We've been there twice already. Our seats are great. We feel like we're on a plane. There are lights overhead that you can turn on and off, and the seats move back and forth. When we get to Grand Central Station in New York City, we'll meet Stacey!

I love you!
— Kristy!

Meet Stacey? Ha. Kristy showed me that postcard and I'm sure my friends *meant* to meet me as planned — but it didn't quite work out that way.

I practically killed myself getting inside the station and rushing to the information booth, which was where we were supposed to meet. I made a point of getting there five minutes ahead of time, just in *case* their train was early. (An early train is a real miracle.) Their train was due at 11:25. I reached the booth at 11:20.

You can't miss the booth. It's in the middle of the main room at Grand Central, and says INFORMATION as plain as day. You can't miss the main room, either. All these constellations and things are painted on the ceiling. It's beautiful and unusual.

I stood around the booth, alternately watching the people and watching the clock.

Eleven twenty-five, 11:30, 11:40.

Where were my friends? I began to feel nervous. Maybe something had happened to them. Maybe their train was late. Or maybe they hadn't come after all. I considered calling Mom and asking her if they had tried to reach me at home. Right away, I decided not to do that. If they *hadn't* called, Mom would probably alert the police.

I waited five more minutes, then turned around and asked a woman in the information booth if there were any reports of delayed trains.

The woman shook her head. Then she asked, "Which train are you waiting for?"

I told her.

"Nope," she said, frowning. "That was right on time."

"Uh-oh."

"Were you supposed to meet someone?"

I nodded. "My friends. We were supposed to meet right here. They've never been to New York alone before."

"This is a big station. I'm sure they're around somewhere," said the woman kindly: "They probably just got mixed up. Or maybe they discovered all the stores here."

As I've said, it would be hard *not* to find the main room and the information booth, but it was possible. For all I knew, my friends were wandering around underground, in the subway tunnels or something.

(If they were shopping, I would kill them.)

I tried to figure out what to do next. I thanked the woman and stepped away from the booth. I looked out at the room. It was crowded, but not too crowded. My friends definitely were not there. I was just about to ask the woman if she could page them, when I heard, "Stacey!"

It was Claudia's voice, but I couldn't see her.

"Stacey!" she called again.

I turned around. My friends were struggling down the steps that lead from one of the outside entrances to the station. Where on earth had they been?

"Where on earth have you been?" I cried as I dashed to them. Since I already sounded like my mother, I went ahead and added, "I was worried sick!"

"We're sorry, we're sorry," Claudia replied breathlessly. She had a suitcase the size of a boxcar with her.

For a moment, I forgot about the botched-up plans. I just looked at those four familiar faces rushing toward me. There was Mary Anne, grinning and looking excited beyond belief; Kristy with a smile a mile wide; Dawn, who seemed to be trying to cover up sheer terror with a tight-lipped smile; and Claudia, who managed to appear both happy to see me and ready to strangle her suitcase.

We met at the bottom of the marble stairs and all tried to hug each other at once.

"Stacey, your hair! It looks fantastic!" exclaimed Claud.

"We've been wandering around, oh, *every*-where!" said Dawn.

"Mary Anne, I love your shirt!" I told her.

"I can't believe I'm here!" she replied.

"What's to eat?" asked Kristy.

"Where have you been?" I asked again.

I led my friends away from the stairs and they put their things down. Kristy and Dawn were each carrying a knapsack. Mary Anne was carrying a small duffel bag. But Claudia had that boxcar.

"What's *in* that?" I wanted to know.

"What should I answer first?" Claud replied. " 'Where have you been?' or 'What's *in* that?' "

" 'What's *in* that?' "

We were all giggling. This was like old times. But I have to admit that I felt sort of . . . conspicu-ous. My friends were making a lot of noise, there was Claudia's suitcase, Kristy was wearing a baseball cap with a picture of a collie on it, Dawn was looking around as if she expected someone to murder us any second, and Mary Anne had just pulled a giant map and guidebook to the city out of her purse.

"Put that away!" I whispered loudly to her. "You look like a tourist."

"Well, I am one."

"But I'm not. Come on. Put it away. We don't want people to think we don't know where we're going. That makes us easy targets."

"For what?" asked Dawn nervously.

"For — never mind," I said, feeling exasperated. What was with Dawn anyway? She's usually so cool.

"I thought you wanted to know what was in my suitcase," said Claudia.

"I do," I told her.

"My clothes," she replied.

"For how long? The next two years?"

"*No*," she said testily. "The next two days."

I should have known. Once, my friends and I went on a trip to the Bahamas and Disney World. Claudia brought almost her whole closet with her.

"And where were you guys?" I asked.

Kristy took over. "I'm not sure," she replied honestly. "When we got off the train, we just kept following people, and after we went up this escalator, we walked through a building and found ourselves outside."

I didn't say anything, but to get *to* the escalators they had to have been in the main room — which meant they walked right near the information booth. And what possessed them to go on an escalator anyway? I hadn't said anything about going on an escalator. Oh, well. It was over now. And we were together.

I drew in a deep breath, let it out slowly, smiled, and said, "So what do you want to do first?"

"Well," Mary Anne spoke up instantly, "I'd love to see Central Park. It's eight hundred and forty-three acres of fun. Or maybe we could go to South Street Seaport, located in the Wall Street area of lower Manhattan and featuring nineteenth-century buildings, three piers, and a maritime museum." Mary Anne grinned smugly. She looked quite proud of herself.

How did she do that? I wondered. She was a walking guidebook.

Kristy noticed the look on my face and said, "I don't get it, either. She talked like that during the entire train trip, and I never even saw the guidebook."

Mary Anne made a face at Kristy. "Maybe we should just go eat lunch," she suggested. "How about the Hard Rock Cafe? It features all kinds of —"

"The Hard Rock Cafe?" repeated Dawn. "Is that in a safe neighborhood?"

I looked at Dawn curiously. Where was all that self-confidence? "Dawn? You okay?" I asked her.

"Oh, sure. It's just that I've never been to New York before," she reminded me. "And it's not as if I lived in a city when we were in California. We lived *outside* of Anaheim — in this teeny little suburb. It just happened to be near Disneyland and some other fun places. But last night? I was listening to the news and I heard about these two murders in New York, and then this building collapsed and crushed someone."

"And *then*," added Kristy, "someone fell down an open manhole and was attacked and eaten by alligators and sewer rats."

"Really?" said Dawn, her eyes widening.

"I'm making it up!" cried Kristy.

"You are? But I've heard that there *are* alligators in the sewers. And pickpockets —"

"In the sewers?" asked Kristy.

"No. On the streets. And chain snatchers and purse snatchers and rats and cockroaches."

Uh-oh.

"How about lunch?" I said. "You guys must be starving. I think the Hard Rock Cafe is a good suggestion. We can hop on a bus —"

"With *this*?" asked Claudia, pointing to her suitcase.

I groaned. The suitcase probably wouldn't fit on a bus, or through the front door of the Hard Rock Cafe for that matter. "I guess we'll have to go back to my apartment first and drop that off," I said. "Of course, it's entirely out of the way."

Claudia looked all huffy. "Couldn't we leave it somewhere?" she asked. "In a locker or something?"

"Not if you want to get it back," I told her. "We'll have to hail a cab, have the driver put that thing in the trunk, which by the way means we'll have to give the driver a huge tip, take it to my building, and then take a bus back to the restaurant."

"I'll pay for the cab," said Claudia contritely. She reached out for a handle on the end of her suitcase and began pulling it toward the stairs. The suitcase was on little wheels. I wanted to die. How embarrassing. Why hadn't I noticed the wheels before? Only grandmothers pull around suitcases on wheels.

Somehow we managed to get up the stairs and out of the building. No sooner had we walked out the door than Dawn screamed.

"What? What is it?" I asked.

"Th-*that!*" Dawn was pointing to a pile of garbage — and a pink tail.

The tail moved. It was attached to a tiny mouse.

Kristy started to laugh, and Mary Anne poked her.

I ignored all of them and hailed a cab.

The cabbie (who was very nice) loaded Claudia's suitcase into the trunk, and then my friends and I piled into the cab. They squished into the backseat and I sat up front with Philippe (the driver). When we got to my building, the doormen were kind enough to let us leave the suitcase behind the front desk, so at least we didn't have to go upstairs. Then Kristy, Mary Anne, and Dawn decided to leave their knapsacks and the duffel bag behind, too, which made sense.

At last we were on our way to the Hard Rock Cafe.

CHAPTER 4

Dear Jeff,

   Is New York ever scary. I'm not sure you'd like it here. It's all cramped and crowded. That's what happens when you try to cram eight million people into such a small area. To make up for it, New Yorkers just keep building taller skyscrapers. Fifty years from now, people will probably have apartments on the three-hundredth floor. Today I saw a gigantic rat — and I seemed much more scared of it than it seemed scared of me!

Your terrified sister,

Dawn

"Oh, my lord!" cried Claudia. "Look at that! Look at *that*!"

We had reached the Hard Rock Cafe and were standing outside. I have to admit that the front of the restaurant is pretty spectacular. There's this wild Cadillac (just half of it) suspended over the entrance, and the license plate reads "God is my co-pilot."

It is extremely cool.

But I wished my friends weren't quite so loud in their admiration of the Cadillac. They were making a lot of noise again and sounded like tourists.

"Did you make a reservation?" asked Mary Anne.

I shook my head. "You can't. They don't take reservations."

"Oh, I hope we can get in," said Kristy, still gazing at the Cadillac.

"We'll get in," I told her. "But we might have a little wait. If this were the weekend, though, we'd probably have to wait in a forty-minute line outside. Come on."

"Forty minutes," I heard Dawn mutter in amazement as my friends followed me inside.

I approached the man who was behind a desk near the doorway and said, "Five for lunch, please."

"Oh, you sound so grown-*up*!" squealed Mary Anne.

(I wanted to kill her.)

"That'll be about five minutes," said the man. "Why don't you just step aside, and someone will seat you shortly."

"Okay," I said. "Thanks."

The five of us stood around and gazed at the restaurant. There's an awful lot to see.

"It's everything I dreamed it would be," said Mary Anne with a sigh.

Claudia and I glanced at each other and smiled.

The restaurant *is* fun to look around. First of all, it's huge. Second, it's a sort of shrine to rock music. There's all this memorabilia hanging on the walls. Things like the Talking Heads' guitars and a poster of David Byrne. Mostly there are a lot of guitars. And signs. Signs everywhere. We were standing right underneath one that said THIS IS NOT HERE. (Kristy started giggling.) Another said WHO DO YOU LOVE? Another said LOVE ALL SERVE ALL. And everywhere — on the menus, the walls — were the words SAVE THE PLANET.

"It's kind of nineteen sixties, isn't it?" commented Dawn.

"Actually," began Mary Anne, "the Hard Rock Café — and I might add that there are Hard

33

Rock Cafes located in Dallas, London, Tokyo, Stockholm —"

I don't know what point Mary Anne was about to make, but luckily she was interrupted by a man who showed us to a table. He seated us right under this glass case which held a wild pair of black-and-white checked platform boots. Under the boots was a brass plaque that read CHUBBY CHECKER.

"Chubby Checker?" Dawn said as we sat down.

Every last one of us shrugged, even Mary Anne, although I'd been certain she was going to open her mouth and say something like, "Chubby Checker. Didn't you know? That was a group that used to sing backup for Elvis Presley in nineteen fifty-six," or something.

But she didn't. Instead, a young woman whose nametag said Meddows came over and handed us our menus.

"Oh, this is so exciting!" exclaimed Mary Anne.

It was only 1:20, and already Mary Anne had said that at least six thousand times. I hoped she would stop.

We studied the menus and then Meddows returned to take our orders.

"I'll have the Poppied Fruit and Avocado

Salad, please," said Dawn, and added, "It sounds so Californian."

"I'll have the 'Pig' Sandwich, please," said Claudia.

"Me, too," said Mary Anne.

"I'd like the Chef's Salad," I said.

"And I," Kristy began, "will have the fill-it mig-nun."

"The *what*?" I said with a gasp.

Meddows smiled. "I know what she means," she said. She scribbled something on her pad. Then we all ordered sodas and she left.

"*Kristy*," I whispered loudly, leaning across the table, "that is pronounced 'fillay meenyon,' *not* 'fill-it mig-nun.'"

"*Sorry*," said Kristy crossly.

I was mortified. There we were in one of the coolest restaurants in all of New York City, a cool waitress to go with it, and Kristy had just ordered fill-it mig-nun.

I wanted to die. I wanted to crawl under the table and *die*.

Somehow we got through lunch and paid for our meal. But we didn't leave right away. There was a little stand near the exit to the restaurant selling Hard Rock Cafe T-shirts and sweatshirts.

"Ooh, look!" said Mary Anne breathily. "A store! I've just got to buy a T-shirt for Logan. That will be the perfect souvenir for him. I promised him a New York souvenir."

So Mary Anne bought a T-shirt for Logan and one for herself, and then Kristy, Claudia, and Dawn bought T-shirts for themselves and for Mallory and Jessi. They even talked *me* into buying one.

"These can be, like, our club uniform!" exclaimed Kristy. "We can wear our shirts to meetings."

"Oh, wow, that will be so cool!" said Mary Anne.

I looked around for a place to hide, but there was none.

We stepped outside. We had walked exactly four feet when a shabbily dressed man planted himself in front of us. We tried to go around him. He blocked our way.

"Oh, no," moaned Dawn.

The man held out a paper cup. "Spare a quarter, ladies?" he asked.

Mary Anne looked at me questioningly.

But Kristy immediately opened up her purse and pulled out her wallet.

I shoved her wallet back in her purse, closed the purse, and steered my friends clear of the man. "*Never* open your purse in the middle of the sidewalk, especially not when someone asks you for money," I snapped.

"But that poor man —" Kristy began, looking over her shoulder at him.

"I know," I said more gently. "I feel bad for him, too. But opening up your purse is a great way to get robbed. Someone could have just grabbed your wallet and run. You guys are in New York now, so watch yourselves. You have to be on your toes."

Dawn turned so pale I thought she was going to faint.

Mary Anne changed the subject. "So where are we going now?" she asked. "I thought we could go to Bloomingdale's, and then maybe to the Museum of Modern Art. You wanted to go there, right, Claudia? And after that —"

"Whoa," I interrupted her. "Wait a minute. It's much later than I thought it would be by the time we finished lunch." (I didn't add that this was because we'd wasted so much time trying to meet each other and then struggling with Claudia's boxcar.) "We've only got time to do one more thing, I think. Then we have to go back to my apartment and get ready for the party. Oh, and there's something else we have to do, but I'll explain about that later."

"Time for just one more thing?" said Claud in disappointment. "Well, I suppose I'm the only one who wants to go to the museum."

She was right. Everyone else wanted to go shopping, so we ended up heading for Bloomingdale's.

In all honesty, I have to say that although Bloomie's used to be my favorite department store, I had recently realized that it is always crowded and always hot. It could be ten degrees outside, but in Bloomingdale's it would be two hundred and thirty-six.

My friends were completely in awe of the store, though. More in awe than they'd been of the Hard Rock Cafe. This was understandable. Bloomingdale's is huge. I've actually gotten lost in it. And there's so much to see, you hardly know where to look. Counter after counter and rack after rack spreads before you. There's jewelry, clothing, fur coats, lingerie, toys, furniture, housewares, electronics. People come after you, offering samples or telling you about specials. It can actually be a little overwhelming.

We wandered through the makeup department and let a woman spray us with perfume. Then we sniffed at our violet-scented wrists and felt very adult. That was pretty much the last good moment of the shopping adventure.

The next thing I knew, this store detective had come after Mary Anne. He demanded to look in her purse. When she opened it, he pulled out a half-used jar of eye shadow.

"I believe this belongs at the Clinique counter," he said.

"I th-thought it was a sample," Mary Anne stammered.

(Everyone was looking at us.)

"You're supposed to try the makeup at the counter, not pocket it," I told her.

The man was very nice and let us go, saying not to let it happen again. I'm sure he thought we were tourist kids from the sticks. (He was four-fifths right.)

After that embarrassing incident, Dawn tripped trying to get on a down escalator and nearly started an avalanche of people. And everywhere we went, Kristy kept exclaiming things like, "Look how *expensive* this is! In Stoneybrook it would only cost half as much," or "Mary Anne, come here. Look at this — a *hundred* and *sixty* dollars for *one* pair of *shoes!*"

I decided that if we got out of the store alive, we could call the afternoon a success.

CHAPTER 5

Dear Mom, Dad, Mimi and Janine —

Hi! How are you. I'm fine. New york is so so cool. The peopel are so so cool too everyone is dressed like magazin modles. We whent to a restarant called the hard rock caffe and we whent to Blomingdals. I bought a pair of baggy sox and Mary Ann allmost got arested but don't tell her father. We also met the kids we'll be siting for tomorrow. Tonight Stacey is having a party for us at her apratment.

Love ya.
Claudia

The one other thing my friends and I had to do before we got ready for the party was go around my apartment building and meet the families whose kids we'd be taking care of the next day. I'd promised the parents we'd do that. They were a little concerned, and I could understand why. I mean, they didn't know my friends, and just because I'd said the five of us used to be in a baby-sitting business together was no real reason to trust Kristy, Mary Anne, Claudia, and Dawn. But they trusted me. All they wanted to do was meet my friends.

So after our safe return from Bloomingdale's, the five of us left our things in my bedroom and then headed for the twentieth floor of my building. I thought we could start at the top and work down.

"Bye, Mom!" I called as I ushered my friends into the hallway.

"Bye, girls!" my mother replied. "Have fun and be careful!"

"No problem!"

I punched the elevator button and we waited.

"Couldn't we take the stairs?" asked Dawn after a moment.

I shook my head. "If we took the stairs from

here to the twentieth floor we'd never be able to walk again."

"But . . . well, have you ever gotten stuck in the elevator?" Dawn wanted to know. "It took a long time for the doors to open when we came up to your apartment."

"Never," I told her firmly. "I have never been stuck. You aren't claustrophobic, are you?"

"She's just a worrywart," said Kristy. "For heaven's sake, Dawn, I can think of worse things than getting *stuck* in an elevator. What if the cable broke and the elevator crashed all the way to the basement?"

"Kristy!" exclaimed Claudia, Mary Anne, and I. (Dawn was speechless with fear.)

The elevator arrived and we convinced Dawn to get on it. We rode to the twentieth floor. Uneventfully, I might add.

The twentieth floor is the top floor of my building. Like most older apartment buildings, it's not *just* the top floor, though — it's the penthouse. (It's owned by Mr. and Mrs. Reames.) Unlike my floor, where there are six apartments, the penthouse is *one* apartment that takes up the *entire* story. As you can imagine, it's huge. It's bigger than the whole *house* my parents and

I lived in in Connecticut. If you took our second story and laid it down next to the first, all that space would still be less than the space the Reameses have.

Another thing about the penthouse — the elevator lets you off in the Reameses' front hall, which is decorated with paintings and vases and stuff. Also an umbrella stand. Of course, the door between the hallway and the Reameses' actual apartment has about thirty-five locks on it, but getting off in *their* hall is a lot nicer than getting off in *ours*, which is dark and has nothing in it but the doors to the apartments and the trash compactor chute.

"Okay," I whispered as the elevator doors opened and we stepped into the Reameses' hallway. "This is the penthouse. It's the biggest, most expensive apartment in the building. The Reameses are really rich. They're *nice*, but rich. So don't touch anything."

"Should we have fun and be careful?" asked Claudia slyly.

"Just be careful. Now, there's only one kid here. Leslie Reames. She's four. And she's a little like Jenny Prezzioso, so be prepared."

"Another spoiled brat?" wailed Mary Anne.

"A *picky* brat . . . But not a bad kid."

I rang the Reameses' bell. Their maid answered.

"Hi, Martha," I said.

"Hello, Stacey," she replied. "Come on in. Leslie's dying to see you."

We stepped inside and every single one of my friends gasped. Kristy even said, "Will you look at this place? It's like a museum."

I think Martha pretended not to hear her.

The Reameses' apartment *is* like a museum. It's even more opulent than the fancy houses in Kristy's neighborhood. My friends were falling all over themselves in a very embarrassing way. You'd think they'd never seen antiques before.

"Stacey! Stacey!"

Little Leslie Reames came tearing through all those antiques and flung herself at me. When I say *little* Leslie, I mean little. Leslie was premature — she weighed less than four pounds when she was born — and she's never caught up with kids her age, size-wise. She's teeny, like a spider, with spindly arms and legs. However, she makes up for her size by having a mouth that rivals Kristy's.

"Hiya, Leslie," I said. I swung her into the air and she squealed.

Mr. and Mrs. Reames came into the living

44

room then and the introductions began. When we were finished, the Reameses spouted their Leslie list, which I've heard a thousand times already.

"Remember her wheat allergy," said Mrs. Reames.

"And she *must* wear a jacket at all times tomorrow," said Mr. Reames.

"Even indoors?" I heard Kristy whisper to Mary Anne.

"No prolonged running," added Mrs. Reames.

And then Leslie spoke up: "And keep me away from dogs."

My friends must have passed the Reameses' inspection, because when we left, Mr. Reames said, "Martha will drop Leslie off at your apartment at about a quarter to twelve tomorrow, Anastasia."

(Mr. Reames may be nice, but he's the only person in the world who would even *think* of calling me by my full first name.)

I was lucky. My friends kept their mouths shut until we were on the elevator, the doors had closed behind us, and we'd started to move.

"Whoa!" exclaimed Mary Anne. "Wheat allergies."

"No prolonged *running*?" cried Dawn, momentarily forgetting that she was on an elevator.

"Worrywarts of the world unite!" added Claudia.

And Kristy said, "ANASTASIA!" She laughed until she cried. She slumped to the elevator floor. The rest of us had to drag her to her feet as we reached eighteen and the doors opened.

"Now, calm down," I whispered loudly as we approached apartment 18E. We were on a normal floor, under a normal buzzing fluorescent light, ringing the bell of a normal apartment.

An attractive Black woman answered the door.

"Hi, Mrs. Walker," I said. "I brought my friends to meet Henry and Grace."

Mrs. Walker smiled and showed us into an apartment that was laid out exactly the same way as ours. But boy did it look different. Both Mr. and Mrs. Walker are artists and they work at home. (They turned their dining room into a studio.) Their apartment is filled with modern art — paintings and sculptures and wall hangings. Some of it I like, some I don't like. (Or maybe I just don't understand it.)

"Henry! Grace!" Mrs. Walker called as Kristy, Dawn, Claudia, Mary Anne, and I gathered in the Walkers' living room.

A few moments later, two little kids peered at us around the kitchen doorway.

"They're shy," I whispered to my friends. Then I spoke up. "Guess what we're going to do tomorrow, you guys," I said. "We're going to go to the museum and see the dinosaurs. And after that, maybe we'll go to the park."

The kids' faces lit up. They stepped out of the kitchen.

"These are my friends," I told Henry and Grace. I introduced everybody. "Henry is five and Grace is three," I added.

Grace nodded and held up three fingers.

"I'm going on six," Henry said softly.

Mr. Walker came out of the studio then. He was paint-covered, and I knew we'd interrupted him, but he just smiled and then he and his wife talked to us baby-sitters for a while.

Fifteen minutes later, we were back on the elevator, and Mary Anne was looking star-struck. "I can't believe it," she said. "Mrs. Walker illustrates books. I met a celebrity!"

"Did you see that painting over their couch?" exclaimed Claudia. "It was fantastic. I wish I could talk about art with the Walkers sometime. Mr. Walker has even had his own show here in New York. Do you know how *major* that is?"

We agreed that a show was major but didn't

really have time to talk about it, since our next stop was just two floors down, on sixteen.

"The Upchurches," I told my friends. "Two girls. Natalie is ten and Peggie is eight. Natalie will be the oldest kid in the group tomorrow. Wait till you see the Upchurches' apartment. Oh, but don't say anything about it, you guys. And there's no Mrs. Upchurch. The parents are divorced and the kids live with their father, okay?"

"Okay," said Kristy, who usually assumes that people mean *her* when they say not to mention something.

I just knew the Upchurch girls would surprise my friends — and they did. They are smart, worldly New York kids. They're not sassy, they're just sophisticated, I guess. (They're probably a lot like I was when I was younger.)

Natalie answered the bell and us baby-sitters walked speechlessly into the apartment. It's decorated entirely in black and white and chrome, and is exceedingly ugly. Having been told not to comment on it, my friends didn't know what *to* say. Luckily, Mr. Upchurch sat us down, so we talked about our sitting experiences and what we planned to do the next day.

Then Natalie and Peggie began telling us about the creative theater group they belong to.

"We express emotions through actions," said Peggie.

"We've learned that the theater is really a stage for *life*," added Natalie.

Kristy waited until the five of us were on the elevator before she said, "I hope Peggie and Natalie can handle something as down-to-earth as dead dinosaurs in a museum."

We giggled. Then it was on to the eighth floor, where we met the Barreras — Carlos, who's nine; Blair, who's seven; and Cissy, who's five, knows Leslie Reames, and can't stand her.

"They had a nice, normal apartment," commented Dawn as we headed for the fifth floor, our last stop.

"Aren't there any other celebrities here, Stacey?" asked Mary Anne.

"Mary Anne, this is an apartment building, not Burbank. We're lucky to have Mr. and Mrs. Walker. If you're looking for movie stars, forget it."

"*Sorry*," said Mary Anne huffily, not sounding one bit sorry.

Dennis and Sean Deluca, who are nine and six, were the last kids my friends met that afternoon. The Delucas haven't lived in New York long, so Dennis and Sean were like my friends in some ways — everything was new to them . . . and a lot of things frightened them. I made a mental note not to let Dawn spend much time with the Delucas.

At long last we got back on the elevator and headed up to my floor.

"You know," said Claudia, "it just occurred to me. The weather is beautiful today, and we found all those kids at home, cooped up in their apartments."

"Well, there's no playground nearby," I told her.

"I thought you live near Central Park," said Dawn.

"We do," I replied, "but kids don't go there alone, not even at Natalie's age. It isn't safe. However, that is just what's going to make tomorrow so great. The museum and the park will be a terrific treat for all the kids. Now, come on. Here's my floor. We've got a party to go to!"

CHAPTER 6

Dear Dad and Jigger,

New York is absolutely fabulous. Can we move here? (Just kidding.) We met a true and honest celebrity — two of them actually. Mr. and Mrs. Walker. They're artists. Mr. Walker has had his own show, and Mrs. Walker illustrates books. Now it's time to get ready for Stacey's party. Don't worry — Mr. and Mrs. McGill will both be at home. Tomorrow we take the kids to the American Museum of Natural History and Central Park. I know everything there is to know about the museum

and the park, and I can't wait to
see them again.

Love,
Mary Anne

"Okay," I told my friends, "it's five o'clock. I
invited people for seven, so we have two hours to
get ready. We have to fix the food, choose tapes
to play, and get dressed. Oh, Laine is coming by
in an hour to help us, so maybe we should get
dressed first."

"Laine's coming over early?" asked Claudia.

Laine, if you remember, is my best friend here
in New York. Claudia was my best friend in
Connecticut. Each girl knew about the other, but
they hadn't met. That night would be the first
time. I was certain they would get along, since *I*
like them both so much, although when I thought
about it, I realized that they didn't have much
in common. Laine is *super*-smart, and Claudia
may be smart, but she doesn't do well in school.
Claudia likes arts and crafts, Laine likes foreign
movies; Claudia reads Nancy Drew mysteries,
Laine reads French poetry; Claudia likes junk
food, Laine likes gourmet food. (She has even
eaten pigeon.) Still, since opposites attract, I just

knew Laine and Claudia would hit it off. Besides, they did have one thing in common — me!

"Yes," I answered Claudia. "I wanted you and Laine to get to know each other before the party starts. Plus, Laine always comes over to help whenever anything is going on here."

Claudia just nodded.

"Well, let's get dressed," said Mary Anne.

"Does this mean I have to stand up?" asked Dawn. We were sprawled around in the living room and Dawn looked beat.

"Yup," Mary Anne told her. "Now Kristy, Claudia, and Dawn, you have to wear what Stacey says. So do I."

"What Stacey says?" I repeated as we walked down the hallway to my room. "What do you mean? You guys can wear whatever you want."

"*Oh*, no," said Mary Anne. "No way. This is New York. I want us to dress New York so we fit in."

"Maybe we should wear our Hard Rock Cafe T-shirts," said Kristy. "They're as New York as you can get."

Mary Anne scowled at her. Then she added, "You especially, Kristy. You wear what Stacey says."

"I hope Stacey says jeans, a sweater, a turtleneck, and sneakers, because that's all I brought.

And who made you Fashion Boss of the World, anyway?"

"What if I say to wear a housecoat, platform shoes, and a beanie with a pinwheel on top?" I asked.

"Stacey, this is *serious*," wailed Mary Anne. "We've got to look our best. We're going to meet all your friends. Aren't you worried about what we wear?"

"No," I replied. "But if it'll make you feel better, Mary Anne, I'll tell *you* what to wear. Let's see what you brought." (I glanced at Claudia's boxcar. She had just opened it and about twenty outfits had fallen out.) "And if there's anything you need to borrow," I added, "I'm sure Claudia will have it."

"Stacey," Claudia began coldly, "for your in —"

"Hey, hey," said Dawn. "Everyone, *calm down*. We're wasting time. Just concentrate on getting dressed."

A half hour later we were ready. Well, maybe not ready, but at least we were dressed. Mary Anne looked at all of us (even me) critically.

"Kristy, borrow an outfit from Claudia, okay?" she said.

Kristy was wearing a white turtleneck with little red and blue hearts all over it, a red sweater, jeans, and sneakers.

"Claudia and I are not exactly the same size," said Kristy, who is not only quite short, but completely flat-chested. "Now get off my case."

"Okay, okay. . . . Stacey, is it all right if Kristy wears that tonight?"

"Of *course*," I said.

Mary Anne continued her inspection. Claudia had on the black outfit we'd talked about over the phone so long ago. And she was wearing her hair simply, for once — brushed back from her face and held in place by a white beaded headband. Dawn had chosen an oversized peach-colored sweater-dress, lacy white stockings, and black ballet slippers. I was wearing a short, short yellow dress that flared out just above my hips, white stockings, yellow push-down socks, and these new shoes that my parents hate. It was an interesting outfit, one I'd thought up while we were dressing.

And what was Mary Anne, the fashion plate, wearing? Well, here's a clue. She looked like she'd walked right out of the pages of *Little House on the Prairie*. I had chosen a bright, big-patterned sweater and a pair of black pants for her. She'd looked at them, shaken her head, replaced them in her suitcase, and put on this other outfit — a ruffly white blouse, a long paisley skirt, and these little brown boots. It was very mature and attractive but, well, Mary Anne was the only one of my friends who, when dressed up, actually *looked* like she came from Connecticut. We could tell, though, that the clothes were new and that she really wanted to wear them, so no one said anything to her, despite the grief she'd given us earlier.

"Well," I said brightly. "Everyone passes my inspection. Come on. We better get busy in the kitchen. Except for you, Claud. Why don't you stay here and look through my music. Choose some things to play tonight, okay?"

"Okay," agreed Claudia. I could tell she was pleased that I'd given her such responsibility.

Mary Anne, Dawn, and Kristy followed me into the kitchen. We began opening bags of chips and pretzels, and packages of cheese and candy, and arranging everything in bowls or on plates.

"Mom?" I called. (Mom was home, but she was at her desk in the den, staying clear of things.)

"Yes?" I heard her reply.

"Did you remind Dad about the heros?"

"I called him this afternoon. He'll bring them when he comes home tonight."

"Oh, okay. Thanks!"

The party wasn't actually a dinner party, but I

knew most of my friends wouldn't have eaten and would be hungry — especially the boys.

"Stacey?" said Mary Anne. "What do you do at a New York party?"

I tried not to look exasperated. "Exactly what you do at a Connecticut party," I told her, and was relieved to hear the doorbell. "That must be Laine!" I cried.

Ordinarily the doormen buzz us when someone comes over, and then we go to our intercom and ask who's downstairs. But Laine comes over so often that the doormen know her and let her upstairs without calling us.

I dashed to the hallway. "Laine?" I said before opening the door.

"It's me!"

I opened the door. "Hi! Oh, I'm glad you're here! Come on in and meet my friends."

The six of us gathered in the living room and I introduced everyone. I saved Claudia for last. "And *this*," I said, "is Claudia Kishi. Laine, Claudia. Claudia, Laine."

Laine was taking off her coat and my friends were watching her with interest. I knew they were wondering what she was wearing. . . . Well, even I was surprised.

Laine was beyond chic. She had chosen a short

black dress, black stockings, and simple black flats. On one wrist was a single silver bangle bracelet. On her dress was one of those silver squiggle pins. Her fluffy brown hair was newly curled and perfectly cut. She looked wonderful — like she was already in high school. My friends were speechless. Claudia looked good, too, but well, maybe not as ready for high school. Her hair was long and flowing, and her outfit was wild, but not particularly adult.

"So you're the members of the Baby-sitters Club," said Laine, smiling. "Stacey's told me a lot about you."

"She's told us about you, too," replied Claudia, and added, "You're the one she had the big fight with after she found out she was diabetic, right?"

That was true — Laine and I had had a fight — but what was Claudia doing? I looked at her, aghast.

"And you're the one she had the fight with when your little club almost broke up," Laine countered.

I groaned. This was not a good sign. Not a good sign at all. The party looked like it was going to be a big mistake.

CHAPTER 7

Dear Mom,

Tonight was Stacey's party. It was interesting. We met her friends and they met us. (New York meets Connecticut.) I guess her friends are nice, but it was hard to tell. Did you and your friends ever fight when you were my age? Maybe we can talk about this when I get home. You'll probably receive this card after I get home, anyway. Don't worry. New York isn't a bummer, but the party sort of was.

I love you!

Dawn

P.S. They have to have doormen here to keep the murderers away.

I have to admit that I felt a little sorry for Dawn and also for Kristy that evening. By now you've probably guessed that the party didn't go too well. Every one of my close friends was aggravating me. Mary Anne was being a pest. She kept pretending to be an expert on New York, trying to impress everyone and be all adult and sophisticated. And Claudia and Laine wouldn't stop sniping at each other. Maybe I'd been naive to think that they'd get along. Why should they? Each knew the other was my best friend, so they were *jealous*. I should at least have *suspected* that that might happen.

Now to be honest, Dawn and Kristy were driving me crazy, too. Dawn was just so nervous about everything, and Kristy never thought before she spoke. But I did feel sorry for them by the end of the evening, and you'll see why.

Let me back up, though, to Laine's arrival. I could hardly believe what Claudia had said to her. If she was feeling jealous of Laine, why hadn't she let me know beforehand? Oh, well. She hadn't. Instead, she had sniped at Laine and Laine had sniped back. (She's not one to ignore a snipe attack.)

Dawn, Mary Anne, Kristy, and I had glanced at each other nervously, and I was about to give

Laine a job in the kitchen, when Mary Anne said, "Laine, Stacey says you just moved to the Dakota Apartments, located at Seventy-second Street and Central Park West, built in eighteen eighty-four. Wasn't the movie *Rosemary's Baby* filmed there?"

Laine looked somewhat bewildered. "I — I don't know. I think the story was sort of supposed to take place there or something. I've never seen the movie or read the book, though. I'm not allowed to."

"*Really?*" squealed Mary Anne. "Me neither! I'm not allowed to, either! We have something in common, don't we? Hey, I've heard that some famous people live in the Dakota. Is that true? Do you know them?"

Laine looked at me questioningly. I wanted to crawl under the couch or something. Mary Anne was as excited as a puppy at Chuck Wagon time.

"Well, yes," Laine replied. "John Lennon lived there. And Yoko Ono still does."

Laine mentioned a couple of other stars, and I thought Mary Anne would pass out from the sheer joy of it all.

"Oh! Oh!" she shrieked. "You're kidding, aren't you? No, you're *not* kidding!"

"Lord," Claudia mumbled. Then she spoke

up. "Guess who lives in Stoneybrook, Connecticut, Laine," she said.

"Who?" asked Laine.

"Herbert von Knuffelmacher."

"I — I don't think I know who that is," said Laine.

"Exactly," replied Claudia. "Nobody does."

I had no idea what Claudia was leading up to, and I didn't want to find out.

"Whoa! Look at the time," I exclaimed. "People are going to start showing up before we know it. Claud, would you and Dawn clear off that table in the living room," I said, pointing, "and arrange the paper plates and stuff on it. Let's see. Mary Anne, you open a couple of bottles of soda and set them out by the cups. Oh, and put some ice in the bucket. And, Kristy and Laine, come help me in the kitchen."

Somehow, the next half hour passed uneventfully, although the uneventfulness did turn to silence, which I counteracted with very loud old music by some group my parents used to like called the Doors. Then Dad showed up with the heros — gigantic ones — and all five of my friends and I had to get busy slicing them into manageable little sandwich sizes. We stuck a fancy toothpick in each one to hold it together.

We had just finished when the buzzer buzzed.

"Great!" I exclaimed. "The first guest!"

"I thought I was the first guest," said Laine at the same time that Claudia said, "I thought we were your first guests. Remember us? The Baby-sitters Club?"

I rolled my eyes, thinking, Ooh, touchy, as I ran into the hallway and pressed the TALK button on the intercom. "Yes?" I said.

"Jim Fulton is here," Isaac told me.

"Thanks," I replied. "Oh, and, Isaac, from now on, you can let everyone come up whose name is on that list I gave you. You don't have to buzz each of them."

"Right," replied Isaac. "Have a nice day." (Isaac says that at anytime of day or night.)

"Jim Fulton?" I heard Mary Anne say behind me. "You didn't say there were going to be boys at the party . . . did you?"

"Sure I did. Why?"

"I don't know. . . . New York boys . . ."

"What are you worried about? You've got Logan. You know how to act around guys."

"I guess. What will we talk a —"

The bell rang. I opened the door and found not only Jim Fulton but Read Marcus there. (Read is a girl. Jim and Read have gone out a couple of times.)

"Hi, you guys!" I said. I let them in, put their coats in my bedroom, and then introduced everybody.

Just as I was finishing, the bell rang again. And kept on ringing. For a while, I was busy letting people in and telling them where to put their coats. Aside from Laine and the club members, I had asked about twenty kids to the party. Thirteen of them were boys. This was to even things up a little, so that there wouldn't be too many girls. I thought this was very nice and thoughtful of me. I wasn't trying to set up any of my friends. I just didn't want them to feel like they were sticking out — unattached hicks from Connecticut or something.

When I had let the last guest in, I ventured into the living room. What I found was not your usual party scene. At the beginning of most parties, I've noticed, the boys and girls divide up and stick to separate sides of the room. The girls gossip and the boys do weird things like turn their eyelids inside out. This goes on until people feel comfortable enough to mix.

That night, my friends were divided up, but not boy *versus* girl. Instead, it was New York *versus* Connecticut, with one exception. While Claudia,

Kristy, and Dawn huddled in a corner, and my other friends stuck together by the food table, Mary Anne stood with Jim and Read. She was talking a mile a minute. I was pleased (at least *some* people were mixing) until I got close enough to them to hear what Mary Anne was saying.

"Imagine — first the Empire State Building, one thousand four hundred and seventy-two feet high, was the world's tallest building. Then the Twin Towers of the World Trade Center were completed and *they* were the tallest, but only until nineteen seventy-five. Now something *else* is taller."

"Mm-hmm," Jim and Read murmured politely, and Jim threw me a look that plainly said, "Get us out of here."

Before I could, Mary Anne went on, "So has either of you seen the house at Seventy-five and a half Bedford Street? I bet it's really cool."

"Huh?" said Read.

"You know. The house that's only nine feet six inches wide? Edna St. Vincent Millay once lived there. The poet?"

"Hey, Mary Anne," I jumped in, "I don't think you've had anything to eat yet. Come over here and get a hero."

"But I'm not hungry," protested Mary Anne.

As I pulled her away, I heard Jim whisper to Read, "What a weirdo."

I thought about saying something to Mary Anne, but decided not to. At least, not right then. I didn't want to spoil the party for her. I headed over to my wallflower friends instead.

"You guys," I said to Kristy, Claudia, and Dawn. "What are you doing here?"

"The same thing everyone else is doing over *there*," Dawn whispered, pointing to the rest of the kids, "only there's more of them. . . . And they're having fun."

"Well, don't just stand here. Go *talk*," I said. "Have you forgotten how to? It's really simple. You just open your mouths and let some words out."

"It is *not* that simple and you know it," Kristy whispered.

"It is, too," I replied. I took Kristy by the elbow and led her over to Coby Reese. Coby and I have been friends (not great friends, but good friends) since we were a year old and our mothers used to take us for walks together. Coby is very cute. More important, he's a regular guy who's easy to talk to.

"Hey, Coby," I said. I nudged him away from this other guy, Carl Bahadurian, who was getting ready to prove that if you cross your eyes and someone hits you on your back, your eyes will *not* be permanently crossed. "Coby, this is Kristy Thomas," I said. "She's a big sports fan. Kristy, Coby is the star forward of our basketball team. He holds two school records."

"Really?" Kristy's eyes lit up. She was definitely interested — in a boy! She sure was changing.

I left the two of them alone.

The party limped along. Eventually, my New York friends and my Connecticut friends began to mix. But as the evening wore on, I saw some strange things. I saw Mary Anne walk right up to a group of kids she hadn't even been introduced to and ask them how often they'd ridden the Staten Island Ferry. The kids gave each other "weirdo" looks. I didn't blame them.

I saw Dawn glance nervously out the windows and then ask Read Marcus where the fire escape was.

"There isn't one," Read replied. "The building's too tall for an outside escape. There are fire stairs at each end of the floor."

"Oh," said Dawn. "Thank goodness."

Later, I saw Mary Anne with a small bunch of kids who (for once) didn't look bored. At last, I thought, she's given up quoting statistics. What was she talking about instead?

". . . never been to New York before," she was saying. "She saw a mouse and thought it was a rat! And she was afraid we'd get trapped in the elevator. She even believes there are alligators in the sewers!"

The kids burst out laughing. Then all eyes turned toward Dawn. Unfortunately, Dawn was nearby, and I know she overheard.

Ooh, wait until I get my hands on Mary Anne, I thought.

However, by this time, everyone had loosened up, and a lot of kids were dancing. Guess who'd been dancing longest of all? Kristy and Coby! I couldn't believe it. At least one of the Connecticut girls was fitting in with my other friends.

A fast song ended and a slow one started. Kristy wrapped her arms around Coby's neck and they smiled at each other. And Claudia chose that moment to tap Coby on the shoulder and say, "May I have this dance?"

Kristy drew back in horror. If looks could kill, Claudia would have been dead and buried. Kristy flounced over to the couch and sulked.

It was eleven o'clock by then and kids were starting to leave. One by one they got their coats and drifted out the door. Even Coby, although he did say a special good-bye to Kristy, and they exchanged phone numbers and addresses.

Finally, only Laine and the members of the Baby-sitters Club were left.

We were utterly silent.

CHAPTER 8

Dear Mom, Watson, Charlie,
Sam, and David Michael,
    We are having a blast! Stacey
threw this super-cool party
tonight, and everyone got along
great. I met this terrific guy
named Coby. And we all met
Stacey's New York best friend,
whose name is Laine. Laine and
Claudia are like sisters now.
It's amazing. I can't believe how
easily Mary Anne, Dawn, and
Claudia and I fit right into the
New York scene.

                    Ciao
                    Kristy

I don't think I need to tell you what a bunch of lies Kristy's postcard was. Hardly anyone got along. Laine and Claudia were more like wicked stepsisters than regular sisters, my New York friends thought Mary Anne was a jerk, and thanks to what she'd said, they thought Dawn was a jerk, too. And Kristy and Coby may have hit it off, but Claudia totally spoiled Kristy's evening by butting in on Coby and flirting with him.

After Laine, Claudia, Mary Anne, Dawn, and Kristy and I had looked at each other silently for a few moments, I said brightly, "Wow, what a mess we've got to clean up. Let's get to work."

"Just a sec," Laine interrupted. "You invited me to spend the night with you guys. Do you still want me to?"

"Of course I do," I replied.

"Well, now," Claudia spoke up quickly, "Laine should only have to spend the night here if she wants to. We wouldn't want to force her into anything."

"*I*," said Laine, "am only going to spend the night here if I'm *wanted*."

"You're wanted by me," I said nervously.

"And me," said Kristy.

"And me," said Dawn.

"And me," said Mary Anne.

Claudia said nothing.

"Claudia?" I prompted her.

Still nothing.

"What'd I do to you?" Laine asked Claudia sharply. "I didn't do anything and you act like you hate me."

"You did too do something," Claudia replied haughtily.

"What?"

"Don't you know?"

"No."

"Well, I'm not going to *tell* you."

"Oh, that's mature. You're a jerk."

"And you're a stuck-up snob."

"You know something?" Kristy spoke up. "Laine's right. You *are* a jerk, Claudia."

"Ex*cuse* me?"

"I said, 'You are a jerk, Claudia.'"

"I heard you the first time," Claud snapped.

"Oh. It's just that you said, 'Excuse me,' which usually means you haven't heard properly," Kristy said sweetly.

"Kristy — shut up. Or else tell me why I'm an alleged jerk."

Claudia may not be a great student, but she I picks up words like *alleged* from reading Nancy Drew stories.

"You," said Kristy, "are not an *alleged* jerk, you're an actual jerk. You cut in on Coby and me. We were having a great time and you flirted with him and spoiled the whole evening."

"I did *not* flirt with him!" Claudia cried. "He was the only boy here that I — I wasn't afraid of. And I didn't want to be a wallflower *all* night. No one was asking me to dance."

"It's no wonder," I heard Laine mutter.

What was happening here? I was crushed. I'd wanted so badly for all my good friends to get to know each other and like each other, but they were becoming enemies, even the club members.

"Could — could you guys, um, keep your voices down?" I asked. "If you don't, Mom and Dad are going to come out here and try to help us patch things up."

"We're beyond patching," said Mary Anne.

"Well, let's at least move into the living room," I suggested.

I'd hoped that once we were in the midst of the mess, my friends would start to clean up, and that eventually they'd forget about their problems and we could have a nice slumber party.

I must have been crazy.

No sooner had we set foot in the living room than Dawn — quiet, even-tempered Dawn —

said icily, "Claudia and Laine aren't the only jerks around here." She looked directly at Mary Anne, who, I might add, is her best friend.

"Me?" asked Mary Anne incredulously. "Are you saying I'm a jerk, too?"

"Allegedly," replied Dawn.

"Why?"

"You don't have *any* idea?"

Mary Anne shook her head. I could see her confidence (what there was of it) oozing away. Her eyes grew bright with tears.

"Then try this," said Dawn. "See if it sounds familiar. 'She saw a mouse and thought it was a rat. And she was afraid we'd get trapped in the elevator. She even believes there are alligators in the sewers.' Then imagine a lot of snickering and laughing."

Mary Anne looked at the rug. The tears slipped down her cheeks. She's a champion crier.

Laine looked at everyone disgustedly. "Can we get back to the original issue here?" she said.

I was so confused and upset that I couldn't remember what the original issue was. "Huh?" I replied.

"You asked me to spend the night," Laine said slowly, as if she were speaking to a really little kid.

"Oh. Oh, yeah. Well, you're still invited."

"Thanks," Laine replied. She looked around the living room. Mary Anne was sniffling and wiping her eyes. Dawn was sprawled in an armchair, her feelings apparently wounded for life. And Claudia and Kristy were glaring at each other, archenemies. Occasionally, Claudia's glare would switch to Laine. "Thanks," Laine said to me again, "but I guess I'd rather not. I'm going to call my dad and have him come get me." Then she added under her breath, "A funeral would be more fun than this."

While Laine waited for her father, she helped clean up. The six of us wandered silently around the living room, tossing paper plates and cups and napkins into garbage bags. Then we carried the leftover food into the kitchen. We were wrapping up the remaining hero sandwiches when the buzzer buzzed.

I ran for it. "Yes?" I said.

"Mr. Cummings is here."

"Okay. Thanks. Laine'll be right down."

"Have a nice day."

"Good night, Isaac."

Laine gathered her things together. I walked her into the hallway. "It's been real," she called to Kristy, Claudia, Mary Anne, and Dawn.

"Yeah, real torture," Claud muttered.

"Laine, I'm sorry," I said quietly.

"Don't worry about it," she reassured me. "Everything will get straightened out. I'll call you tomorrow."

The elevator arrived and the doors swallowed her up. She was gone.

I wished I didn't have to go back inside my apartment. Imagine — not wanting to go into your own home. Of course, I did anyway. But I was so mad at all my friends — even Kristy and Dawn, whom I also felt sorry for — that I marched right inside, shut and locked the door behind me, and said firmly, "Kristy and Dawn, you sleep on the sofa bed in the den. Mary Anne and Claudia, you sleep on the sofa bed here in the living room. I'm sleeping in my own bed."

My friends nodded. They got their stuff out of my room. A half hour later, we were ready for bed. Not one of us had spoken since I'd made the bed announcement. I told my friends to gather in the living room.

"Look, you guys," I said. "It's been a long day. It hasn't been a great evening. We're all tired. But I'm calling a truce. The truce has to last until at least tomorrow night. Because tomorrow, we've got ten kids to sit for, and we can't do that if we're not speaking. So, truce?"

"Truce," mumbled Kristy, Mary Anne, Dawn, and Claudia.

As I was walking down the hall to my room, Dawn called after me, "Stacey? Are the doormen on duty all night? And do your locks work? And, oh, by the way, you do have an alarm system, don't you?"

"Yes," I told her, even though the alarm system part wasn't true. Then I went to bed.

CHAPTER 9

Dear Mimi

Remerber when the Babbysiters club took car of forteen children? At Kristy's house. Well today was are day to take car of ten kids what a job that was. We met the kids yesterday, just to say hi to them and today their parnets dropped them of at Stacey's apratment. They all know Stacey but some were confused when they saw the big crowd and their were some tears.

I luv you.
Claudia

When I woke up the next morning I felt pretty subdued. I wondered how the others were feeling.

I had purposely separated Kristy and Claudia, and Dawn and Mary Anne, but I knew that had not solved the real problem.

What *was* the real problem? I lay in bed and thought about it. Maybe there were several problems. I finally decided that was true. In fact, there were three problems:

1. People get out of whack when they're on a trip. Their routine is different and they're spending more time together. Those changes might put them on edge.

2. My Connecticut friends had desperately wanted to impress my New York friends. This was especially important to Mary Anne.

3. Laine and Claudia were jealous of each other, but neither would admit it.

Hey! I thought. We've got a lot of problems here, but none of them are exactly mine.

Although I *am* the host of these people, so it would help (a lot) if everybody could get along.

What I did have to worry about was baby-sitting for ten kids all afternoon. They were going to start showing up around eleven-thirty and it was already nine o'clock. I got out of bed and went to the window, hoping the weather was nice. I peeked outside — a perfect day. The sky (what I could see of it) was a glittering blue, not a cloud in sight. Great. We could take the kids outdoors. Being stuck indoors in one apartment with ten children and five squabbling baby-sitters was not my idea of a stellar afternoon.

I tiptoed down the hall and into the living room, where I found a note from my parents saying that they'd gone out for breakfast. Mary Anne and Claudia were still asleep.

I peeked into the den. Kristy and Dawn were awake. Not up, but awake.

"Morning," they said sheepishly.

"Morning," I replied. "How are you feeling? Did you sleep okay?"

"Like a log," Dawn replied. "I didn't think I would. I thought, you know . . ."

"Ghoulies and ghosties?" I supplied, smiling.

"More like burglies and ratties."

"You know," I said, "you do have to be careful here. You have to be careful in any big city. But be reasonable, too. You'll make yourself crazy if you worry about everything."

"I know."

"Besides," added Kristy, "I bet there are things to worry about that you haven't even imagined yet."

"*Kristy*," I said.

"Well, it's true. Like getting food poisoning in a restaurant. Or getting run over by a bus. Or getting bitten by an animal in the petting zoo in Central Park."

I didn't know whether to strangle Kristy or laugh at her. Shaking my head, I left the den to wake up Claudia and Mary Anne. I was beginning to feel edgy again. Was Kristy going to be a pest for the rest of the weekend? Would Dawn worry herself into a frenzy?

"Hey, you guys," I said, gently shaking Claudia and Mary Anne.

The living room, at least the part of the living room around the sofa bed, was a huge mess. I knew most of the mess was Claudia's. Mary Anne is usually fairly neat. (Actually, Claudia is, too. It's just that she had those two years' worth of clothes with her.)

"Rise and shine!" I said cheerfully.

"Ohhh," groaned Claudia. "Please."

I remembered then how I'd hated for my mother to stick her head in my bedroom and say that.

"It's nine o'clock," I informed them. "No, it's nine-oh-six. The children are going to start coming by in about two and a half hours. So we better get up and get going. We've got to make some plans."

"You sound like a cruise director," mumbled Claudia.

My only reply to that was, "Remember our truce."

An hour later, Mom and Dad had returned, and my friends and I had dressed, eaten breakfast, folded up the sofa beds, and tidied the living room, den, and my bedroom. We were sitting around in my room.

"It's kind of like the old days, isn't it?" I said. "This could be a club meeting. My room could be Claudia's room, and I could be the treasurer again —"

Kristy jumped up from where she'd been sitting on the floor, ousted me from my armchair, reached over to my desk, grabbed a pad of paper and a pen, stuck the pen over her ear, and said, "Even though I don't have my visor on, I call a meeting of the Baby-sitters Club."

(In Stoneybrook, Kristy conducts meetings from Claudia's director's chair and always wears a visor and sticks a pencil over one ear.)

Claudia made a rude noise, but Kristy said sharply, *"Truce."* Then she went on, "Remember when we were going to sit for the fourteen kids before my mom got married to Watson? We made a list of all the children, in age order. That was pretty helpful. Let's do that again. Mary Anne, you're the secretary. You make the list. Stacey, go over the names and ages of the kids."

"Okay," I replied. And we got to work. When we were finished, Mary Anne's list looked like this:

Natalie Upchurch – 10
Dennis Deluca – 9
Carlos Barrera – 9
Peggie Upchurch – 8
Blair Barrera – 7
Sean Deluca – 6
Cissy Barrera – 5
Henry Walker – 5
Leslie Reames – 4
Grace Walker – 3

"It does sort of put things in perspective," Dawn commented.

"Maybe we should make name tags," Kristy suggested. "We did that with the fourteen kids, too. Remember how useful they were?"

I shook my head. "No name tags," I said firmly. "It's not a good idea. It's not safe. We don't want strangers to know the kids' names."

"We don't?" Dawn said in a trembly voice.

"Oh, lord," muttered Claudia, giving Dawn an exasperated look.

"TRUCE!" said Kristy, Mary Anne, and I at the same time. If we hadn't all been so edgy, that would have been funny. But none of us laughed. We just shut up.

"So what are we going to do today?" Kristy asked after a little while. "You mentioned the museum and the park, Stacey, but we should have some sort of schedule in mind. Oh, and what time do we bring the kids back? How long is the meeting their parents are going to?

"I don't know exactly," I answered. "I mean, no one does. But Mom said she thought it would be three or four hours. I figure we should bring the kids back between three-thirty and four."

Kristy nodded. Then we decided on a tentative schedule for the afternoon, which included lunch at the museum. (The parents were going to give us money in advance to cover expenses such as food and the admission to the museum.)

At 11:35 the doorbell rang. I looked at my friends. "Well," I said, "this is the beginning: I hope we're up to this."

I really meant that last part. We had conducted our meeting civilly (the truce was working), but that was about all you could say. There hadn't been any laughing or joking or teasing. Just grim business.

"Come on. Let's see who's at the door."

It was Leslie Reames and Martha.

"Good-bye!" Martha called happily as she left Leslie in our doorway. It was Martha's afternoon off, and she looked as if she planned to enjoy it.

Leslie stepped inside. "Remember my wheat allergy," she said. "And not too much running, and I hate dogs."

Us baby-sitters refrained from rolling our eyes.

Unfortunately, the next kids to arrive were the Barreras. It was unfortunate because Cissy dislikes Leslie so much. I couldn't blame Cissy, really, but we'd have to try to keep the girls apart. Cissy is this sturdy, playful tomboy who has no use for delicate, nervous Leslie. She and her brothers are sort of rough and tumble. They're not bullies. They're just lively and full of fun.

Before a fight could break out, though, the Walkers arrived. Peggie and Natalie were right behind them, and a few minutes later the Delucas brought Dennis and Sean by.

Our living room was packed. Mr. and Mrs. Walker and Mr. and Mrs. Deluca hadn't left yet. Henry, Grace, and Sean were in tears, and Leslie was screeching because Carlos Barrera had invited her to come see the Barreras' new puppy. Carlos was trying to be nice; Leslie thought he was being mean.

"It's time to get rid of the adults," I whispered to Kristy.

Before I could say anything, though, my parents came into the living room and announced, "The meeting will start in ten minutes. We better get going."

With difficulty, the Walkers left Henry and Grace, and the Delucas left Sean. The three kids were still crying.

"Have fun and be careful," Mom said to me.

The apartment door closed behind the adults. I locked it. Then I returned to the living room. I looked into the faces of the ten children and four other baby-sitters. Every last one of them looked nervous — no, scared.

CHAPTER 10

Hi, Mal!

Guess what we did today. We went to the American Museum of Natural History. It was so, so cool. You would have loved it. So would your brothers and sisters. Especially the triplets, I think. Dinosaur skeletons everywhere. And big cases showing animals (stuffed ones) in their habitats. But we had a scare. Boy, did we have a scare! We lost one of the kids we were sitting for. We almost panicked...until Mary Anne helped us to remember that a good baby-sitter keeps her head at all times. Anyway, everything turned out fine, of course.

See you at the next club meeting!

Dawn

"Okay," I said. "First things first."

I had decided to take charge, but being in charge felt funny. Kristy was usually in charge. She was the president, the leader, the one with the big ideas. However, I was the only one who knew all these kids, the only one who knew where the museum was, and the only one who knew her way around Central Park. I was also the only one with keys to the apartment *and* the only one of us sitters who was a resident of the building. Therefore, I was the only one the doormen would allow to walk outside with the kids.

I called my friends over. "Kristy," I said, "you keep Leslie and the Barreras apart. Dawn, you and Mary Anne and I will each calm down one of the criers. Claud, you keep an eye on the rest of the kids. As soon as things are under control, we'll leave."

My friends followed the orders, but I could tell that Kristy didn't like doing it. Even so, we were ready to leave in just fifteen minutes. As we were letting the kids out the door, I got a great idea.

"I know how to keep the children together while we walk to the museum," I whispered to the other sitters. I raised my voice and addressed the kids. "How many of you have heard the story about Madeline?" I asked.

All but Grace said, "I have!" (I guess Grace was too young.)

"It's about twelve little girls who do everything in two straight lines," I told Grace. "They sleep in two rows of beds and eat at two sides of a long table. And when they take walks, they walk in two straight lines. That's just what we're going to do. I want each of you to choose a partner and hold hands. Then one of us sitters will walk with each pair. We'll have two lines of kids and one line of sitters. Remember to hold hands."

It worked. We looked like an army drill team, but the kids seemed to like it, even the older ones. They assembled in the hallway. Then Dennis Deluca commanded, "March!" and we marched down the hall. We squished into the elevator. We marched in place while the elevator zoomed to the lobby. We marched out of the elevator and by the doormen.

"Hup, two!" Blair called to Isaac and Lloyd at the desk.

"Have a nice day," Isaac replied.

We marched out the front door, which James held open for us, turned left, and marched up the block toward Central Park West. We passed Judy, the homeless woman.

"Hup, two!" Blair cried cheerfully.

But Judy was in one of her moods. "They'll make you eat rotten vegetables! You have to watch out for those theater people!" she replied bafflingly. She was shrieking at the top of her lungs and Grace began to whimper. But Dawn quieted her down right away.

We reached Central Park West, turned the corner, and marched to the front entrance of the American Museum of Natural History. It was interesting: The baby-sitters were more in awe of the sight of the museum than the kids were. I guess that was because most of the kids pass by the museum at least twice a day, but not my friends. Dawn, Claudia, Mary Anne, and Kristy stopped marching and stood at the wide steps to the main entrance of the great stone building. They gawked.

"Wow," said Mary Anne under her breath. "I've been here before, but I'd forgotten what the museum looks like. It's so . . . so, I don't know, impressive."

"It's beautiful," murmured Dawn.

"Remember that," I told her. "New York isn't just burglies and ratties and pickpockets and trash. It's culture, too. It's museums and art galleries and theaters and architecture."

The children couldn't have cared less about culture, though. As we stood at the bottom of the steps, they began talking and exclaiming.

"Can we go the Naturemax Theater?" asked Carlos. "It's got the biggest movie screen in New York."

"I want to go to the planetarium," said Natalie.

"Yeah, they've got a laser show," said Dennis.

"There's a *Sesame Street* show," added Cissy.

"I just want to see the stars," said Natalie. "They make me feel at one with the universe."

"Huh?" replied every last one of us.

Then Henry spoke up shyly. "Please can we go inside and see the dinosaurs and animals?" he asked.

In the end, that was what we decided to do. The planetarium and the special shows cost extra money, and we didn't have just endless funds. But we could easily afford the general admission to the museum. So we stepped inside, paid our fees, and found a floor plan of the museum. I had brought along a copy of the museum guidebook which Dad had bought the last time we were there. It was really helpful, and us sitters could use it to answer questions the kids might have.

"Where do you want to go first?" I asked the kids.

"Wait, I can't get my button on," said Blair.

We'd each been given a metal button with a picture of an animal skeleton and a human skeleton on it when we'd paid our fee. I helped Blair fasten his button to his shirt collar. "Okay, where to?" I said again.

"Dinosaurs!" cried all the kids except for Peggie, who said, "Gift shop. Puh-*lease*?"

"Before we leave," I told her.

Dawn was studying the floor plan of the museum. "Dinosaurs are on the fourth floor," she informed us.

"Let's go!" I said.

We took an elevator up to four, and right away had to make a decision: Did we want to see the Early Dinosaurs or the Late Dinosaurs?

We started with the early ones and entered a great, high-ceilinged hall. All the kids had been there before, but still they drew in their breaths at the center display in the room. (So did the sitters.) It was really impressive: free-standing, complete skeletons of a stegosaurus, an allosaurus, and best of all, an impressively gigantic brontosaurus.

Henry Walker stood by the brontosaurus and stared and stared. "I wish I could have seen a real bronto," he informed me, sounding as if he were on intimate terms with prehistoric creatures. Grace looked frightened and began to cry, though. I ended up having to carry her around while she hid her eyes in fear of the "monster bones."

After oohing and aahing and looking up some things in the guidebook, we moved into the hall of the Late Dinosaurs, Grace still in my arms. I like the late dinosaurs better. They're so wild-looking. And they have more interesting names.

"Monoclonius," Peggie sounded out.

"Styracosaurus," said Carlos slowly.

Blair's favorite, which he couldn't pronounce, was the corythosaurus, a duck-billed aquatic dinosaur.

Henry stood gawking in front of another display of giant rebuilt skeletons in the middle of the room — two trachodonts, a tyrannosaurus, and a triceratops.

We could barely pull him away from the skeletons, but after about fifteen minutes, the other kids (especially Grace) were ready to move on.

"Please, please, *please* can we go to the fish place?" begged Cissy.

I knew what she meant and why she wanted to go there, and I wanted to go, too, even though the ocean-life stuff was all the way down on the first floor.

"Let's go," I told the other sitters. "There's a

ninety-four-foot replica of a blue whale hanging from the ceiling. It's really amazing. The kids love it."

So we headed down to the first floor. We were no longer in our Madeline lines (we felt funny marching through the museum that way), which may explain how we got all the way to the blue whale before we realized that Henry was missing.

We counted heads three times. We retraced our steps to the elevator. We called for Henry.

No answer. I felt my knees and stomach turn to water. "We've lost a kid!" I cried.

"Oh, my lord!" said Claudia in a horrified voice.

"Now just a sec," said Mary Anne, who usually stays calm in emergencies. "I think each of us should take two kids — well, except for me; I'll just take Natalie since she's the oldest — and search one floor of the museum. Stacey, you go to the lower level. Claud, you stay on this floor. Dawn, you go to two. Kristy, go to three. And Natalie and I will go back to four. Look very carefully and we'll meet at the information booth near the main entrance in fifteen minutes. Got it? If we haven't found Henry by then, we'll tell a guard or an official or someone."

No one argued with Mary Anne. We split up immediately. Sean Deluca and Grace and I searched the restaurants and gift shop on the lower level.

No Henry. When our fifteen minutes were up, we raced to the information booth. I was in a full-fledged panic. I'd never lost a kid before. Why did I have to lose the first one in the middle of New York City?

But my fears dissolved when we stepped off the elevator and walked around the corner. Ahead of us was the information booth. And there were Mary Anne, Natalie, and Henry. I ran to them and hugged Henry. Then Grace hugged her brother — fiercely.

"Thank you, Mary Anne!" I exclaimed. Then I turned to Henry. I was about to scold him when I saw Mary Anne shake her head.

"He went back to find the brontosaurus," she whispered to me, "but he was terrified when he couldn't find *us*. He'll stay with the group now."

The other sitters and kids showed up then, and my friends and I looked at each other. We grinned with relief.

CHAPTER 11

Hi Nannie!
Here I am in New York! They
call it the Big Apple. I don't
know why. Have you ever been
here? We took ten kids to the
American Museum of Natural
History. Then we went to Central
Park. I didn't know there would
be so many things in the park,
but there's a zoo, a merry-go-
round (the Freidman Memorial
Carousel), a boat pond, a statue
of Alice in Wonderland, an ice-
skating rink, and even more. You
can go roller-skating, horseback
riding, bike-riding, boating, or —
Uh-oh, I ran out of room!
                    Love, Kristy

As soon as we'd found Henry, I decided we should leave the museum. We'd been there awhile already, and anyway, the weather was so great I thought the kids would enjoy being outdoors.

We'd forgotten one thing, though. No one had eaten lunch! So we went to Food Express, a huge fast-food restaurant on the lower level of the museum, and ordered burgers or sandwiches and soda. Leslie and Dawn and I had salad, though. Salad is healthier, and for Leslie it's safe because of her wheat allergy. I thought she'd kick and scream at the idea of a salad, but she gobbled it up.

After lunch I was really ready to get outdoors. Unfortunately, a big gift shop is right next to the restaurant, and I *had* promised Peggie we'd go to it. So we went inside and the kids exclaimed over everything, mostly the dinosaur stuff — mugs and T-shirts and puzzles and charts and stuffed animals. It was Dinosaur Heaven. We didn't have enough money to buy souvenirs, though, so we looked around for awhile, then ushered the kids outside empty-handed.

"*Now,*" I announced triumphantly to my friends, "you are going to see the park to end all parks."

"I've been to Central Park before," Mary Anne spoke up.

"Oh, so you've seen the crouching panther statue," I said.

"Huh?"

"And you know where the Dene Shelter is, too, I guess."

"The Dene Shelter?"

"Oh, please, Stacey, can't we do the fun stuff?" cried Cissy.

"Like what?" I teased her.

"Like the zoo."

"I thought the zoo was closed down so they could rebuild it," said Dawn.

"The main zoo is," I told her, "but not the children's zoo."

"Oh, let's go there first!" said Grace. It was one of the few things she'd said all day. Basically, she had just cried about the monster bones. And when Mary Anne had asked her what she wanted for lunch, she'd replied, "A hangaber."

It was quite a walk to the zoo. I mean, a long one. But walking was the fastest and cheapest way to get there. We formed our Madeline lines again in front of the museum, crossed Central Park West, and entered the park, which spread out before us, at Eighty-first Street. Then, heading south and west, we zigzagged through the park, sticking to paths and roads.

My friends couldn't believe what they saw — and what they didn't see.

"Right now," commented Kristy as we walked through a wooded area, "if I couldn't hear traffic, I'd think we were in some great forest. You can't see the city at all."

It was true. We were walking through a thick grove of trees. Leaves crunched under our feet. We could smell earth and evergreen needles, and, well, it's hard to describe, but simply that scent of growing things. I had smelled it in Stoneybrook, oh, and in the Brooklyn Botanical Gardens. But not in too many other places.

We couldn't see any buildings or streets or cars or even people.

At last we emerged from the woods onto a road. Ahead of us was a huge pond. A hot-dog seller had set up his stand by the side of the road.

"Thank heavens," I heard Dawn murmur.

"What?" I asked her. "You hate hot dogs."

Dawn looked embarrassed. "Not that," she replied.

"Did you think we were going to get mugged back there or something?" I said.

"Well, you always hear stories about people getting mugged in Central Park," she said with a little shiver. "And not just at night," she was quick to add when she saw me open my mouth. "Plus, homeless people live in the park, don't they?"

"So?" I replied. "Just because they're homeless doesn't mean they're going to hurt you."

Dawn looked away from me. I think she was going to say something else but she set her mouth in a firm line, stared straight ahead, and marched forward with Natalie and Peggie. Our lines had sort of deteriorated by then, but that was okay. The lines were more useful on the street and in the apartment building. We were still holding hands in groups of three, though, and that seemed safe enough.

We cut across a road and followed a path through what seemed like a more regular park, with trees here and there, benches, playgrounds, a baseball diamond. I barely noticed any of it, since I cut through the park pretty often.

But my friends, and even the kids (who also come to the park pretty often), kept exclaiming over things.

"Look! Look at that man! He's walking . . . *nine* dogs!" cried Sean, after counting them furiously.

"There's a lady feeding pigeons!" said Grace excitedly.

"Yeah, a whole *flock*!" added Henry.

"Oh, my lord, would you look at *that*?" exclaimed Claudia.

I had to admit that what she saw was strange and unusual — even for New York. An old man with a flowing white beard was riding an adult-sized tricycle. Attached to the back of the tricycle was a kid's red wagon. And riding placidly in the wagon were three fluffy white Persian cats. They looked like the man's beard.

"Oh, wow!" I cried.

My friends turned to me with smiles.

"Haven't you seen him before?" asked Kristy.

"No. Well, not for a few years. I'd forgotten about him."

"It's nice to see you get excited about something," said Claudia as we walked along. We'd almost reached the zoo.

"What do you mean?" I asked.

"I mean, you act like there's nothing new or exciting in this city. Like you've seen it all before and so now nothing really matters anymore."

"I do?" I said. That was something to think about.

We were standing in front of the entrance to the children's zoo and were about to pay the admission fee, when Peggie cried, "Oh, the clock! The animals are going to dance!"

The Delacorte Clock. Something else I'd forgotten about. How could I have? Was this what happens when you grow older? Or was I becoming a New York snob? Someone who's lived in the city for so long that she takes everything for granted? And then a jarring thought occurred to me: Maybe my friends were as exasperated with me as I was with them.

I shook myself free of the thought as the fifteen of us ran to the nearby clock tower I used to love when I was a kid. It wasn't just any clock, though. As it struck the hour (I looked at my watch — two o'clock) the circle of statue animals, each holding a musical instrument, began to revolve slowly.

We watched solemnly until the song ended.

Peggie sighed with happiness. (So did I.)

Then we paid the small fee to enter the children's zoo. From the outside, it looks like a blah building. But when you cross through the building and go outdoors again, you find yourself in a storybook land. The animals are housed in brightly painted buildings. There's a castle, a gingerbread house, and even Noah's Ark with a (fake) giraffe's head poking through the roof. And you can pet lots of the animals.

I wished I'd brought my camera along. My friends and I kept pointing at things and giggling.

"Look!" cried Claudia, nudging me.

I glanced up in time to see a goat trying to nibble a piece of paper that was in Blair's back pocket.

We watched Leslie wrinkle her nose up at a bunny rabbit.

We watched Natalie talk to some birds.

"Do you think she's communing with nature?" asked Kristy.

My friends and I burst out laughing. I knew we were feeling more like "our old selves," as my mother would say.

When the kids grew tired of the zoo, I decided it was time for a rest — and maybe dessert. Lots of vendors were around, and it was hard to pass up every one we saw.

"Who wants dessert?" I asked the kids as we left the zoo and came across an ice-cream vendor, a popcorn vendor, and a toy vendor.

Dumb question. The kids wanted *every*thing. The toys were too expensive, but we bought thirteen dixie cups (no ice cream for me or Dawn) and two giant boxes of popcorn. Then we sat down on some wide, flat rocks and ate . . . and ate.

"Stacey?" said Leslie when we were finished. "I don't feel too good."

Uh-oh, I thought. I can't *stand* to see people barf.

Dawn remembered that. Without my saying a

word, she took Leslie aside. She rocked her and talked to her quietly. Ten minutes later, Leslie hopped up and announced, "Okay! I'm all better! Let's go!"

Another crisis had passed.

"Thank you, Dawn," I said gratefully. "You know how I feel about . . ."

"The B-word?" suggested Dawn. We laughed. "I may be nervous about the city," she went on, "but I can handle a little, um, B. Anyway, she didn't get sick."

"But she might have," I said, shuddering.

"Hey, let's get going!" cried Mary Anne. "There's a whole park to explore, and we've got to take these kids home in an hour or so."

By now we were so relaxed that we let the kids run ahead of us. My friends and I linked arms and followed them. The Baby-sitters Club was together again.

CHAPTER 12

Dear Janine —

Hi, how are you? I'me fine. We whent to Centrle park today and saw a clock and whent to the childrens zoo. Remerber when you read Stewart little to me we saw the boat pond where he had his scarry advertiure. We saw a stachew of Alice in wonderland. The kids climed all over it. They were allowed to. I'll be home by the time you get this post-crad. I hop you had a good weekend.

Love,

your sister Claudia

It had been a long time since I'd just wandered through the park. Usually my friends and I go tearing through it to get to the east side of the city. I hardly ever wander around looking, the way I used to do when I was a kid.

But that was how we spent the rest of our time in the park. First we ambled west until we came to —

"The merry-go-round!" Leslie shrieked. "There it is! Please please please please please can we ride it?" She jumped up and down on those little legs of hers that looked like they couldn't support a mosquito.

The carousel costs next to nothing to ride, so I paid for the ten kids. Then, as an afterthought, I gave the man enough money for five more fares.

"Come on, you guys," I said to the members of the Baby-sitters Club. "We're riding, too."

My friends looked doubtful at first. Then they grinned and scrambled for horses. So there we were, bobbing up and down on a carousel in the middle of a park. I felt like I was in *Mary Poppins* (which, by the way, is my favorite movie ever). It was as if Mary Poppins and Jane and Michael Banks and I had jumped into one of Bert's chalk drawings on a London sidewalk and were riding the carousel in a make-believe world.

"Stacey?" said Mary Anne, interrupting my daydream.

"Yeah?" (I was afraid she was going to spout some fact, like how old the carousel was, or how much it had cost to create, or how many horses were on it.)

But all she said was, "This is really fun. I'm glad we came to the park today."

"Me, too," I replied.

The carousel wound down, and the older kids reluctantly slid off their horses. My friends and I helped the younger ones climb down, and then we set off again.

"I didn't know the park was so big," commented Kristy.

"And you haven't even seen half of it," I told her.

"Here are the checker-people!" called Henry suddenly.

"The checker-people?" I repeated, and then I realized what he meant. We'd come to a group of tables, sort of like picnic tables — with benches attached to the sides. Only these tables aren't as long as picnic tables and the tops are very special. They've got checkerboards built right into them. A lot of old people, and some not-so-old people, bring their checkers or chess sets to the tables in nice weather and enjoy games and company.

Blair Barrera tugged at my hand. I looked down at him.

He indicated that he wanted to whisper something to me, so I leaned over.

"They're very serious," he said, nodding toward Henry's checker-people.

He was right. A lot of the players had brought along clocks or stopwatches so they could put time limits on their moves. They sat at those tables in silence, concentrating as hard as if they were taking IQ tests.

So the players were not pleased when Leslie suddenly shrieked, "Cut it out! Stop that, Cissy. *Stop* that! You are an old toad!"

"I am not. You are," Cissy retorted. "Because I'm rubber and you're glue, and whatever you say bounces off me and sticks to you. Nyah, nyah, nyah."

"Unh-unh," sang Leslie, hands on hips. "*I'm* rubber and *you're* glue."

"No, *I'm* rubber —"

"You guys!" I cried desperately.

Four checkers players and two chess players were glaring at us. I felt as if we had just screamed in a library.

"Come on," I whispered to my friends. "Let's get the kids out of here."

We hurried along a path that wound down a little hill, and found ourselves in a wide-open area. A group of kids were playing softball. Two guys were tossing a Frisbee back and forth.

Claudia burst out laughing.

"What?" I asked.

"There's a *dog* playing Frisbee!" she cried, pointing to a German shepherd just as it leaped into the air, expertly catching a Frisbee thrown by its master. "And it's a better player than I am!"

We walked and walked. By the time we reached the boat pond, the kids were looking tired and us baby-sitters were feeling tired. We sat down on some benches. There was plenty to watch. For one thing, this golden retriever kept diving into the pond for a swim, leaping out, shaking himself off all over whoever was nearby, and diving in again.

Then Carlos spoke up. "I wish I had my boat with me."

"Do you have one of *those* boats?" asked Dennis enviously.

"Those" boats are specially powered sailboats and sloops that can be controlled from the shore. Their owners turn them loose in the pond and then direct them here and there, running back and forth at the edge of the water, making the boats zigzag and loop, using the remote controls to keep them from crashing into each other. They're sort of like bumper cars, except you can't ride in them; you can only watch.

"Sure I've got one," replied Carlos. "Don't you?"

"No," said Dennis. "I want one, though. Has yours ever been in an accident?"

"Only about a million of them. It survived."

"Like Stuart Little," added Peggie Upchurch.

"Who's Stuart Little?" asked Sean.

"Who's Stuart Little?" repeated Peggie, looking alarmed.

"Peggie, not everyone reads as much as you do," said her older sister.

"I read plenty!" protested Sean.

"Then you should know who Stuart Little is," said Peggie.

"*I* don't know who he is," spoke up Leslie.

"Me neither," said Grace softly.

"Perfect," I replied. "Then I'll tell you who he is. He's a mouse. A man named E. B. White wrote a book about him."

"Is he real?" asked Leslie, wide-eyed.

"Who? E. B. White?" said Kristy.

"No! Stuart Little."

"He's made up," Kristy told her, and pulled Leslie into her lap for the story.

"Stuart," I began, "was sort of a surprise. He was a mouse who was born to human parents,

Mr. and Mrs. Little. They were expecting a baby, of course, but they got this mouse. The Little family lived right here in New York City, and one day Stuart took himself over here, to this very pond."

I told the kids about Stuart's adventure in the pond, and the wind that blew up, and his scare. Even the kids, like Peggie, who had heard or read the story several times already, listened dreamily. (Partly because they were tired, I think, but who cares?)

When I finished the story I said, "I think it's time to start for home, kids. We don't have to be back for a while, but we've got to walk all the way through the park again, and that's going to take some time."

"Aw, Stacey, do we *have* to?" whined Cissy.

"Yes, we do," I told her. I wasn't sure if she was whining because she didn't want to leave the park or because she didn't want to walk home. At any rate, I told her to climb up for a piggyback ride. Kristy did the same with Grace, Dawn did the same with Leslie, Mary Anne did the same with Henry, and Claudia did the same with Sean. We set off.

Soon we stopped by the Alice in Wonderland statue and let the kids climb on it. Then we walked on. We passed roller skaters and a man who was performing magic tricks. But we never saw the crouching panther. I'd forgotten where it was; I remembered only that it was on a route Laine and I used to take when we would rent skates and go careening around the park.

By the time we were nearing the west side of the park and Eighty-first Street, the piggyback riders were walking again and the ten kids were ahead of us baby-sitters. They were huddling together and whispering.

"They're up to something," I said to Claud, nudging her. "I just know it."

"Well, we're lucky," she replied. "Whatever it is, it's quiet."

Famous last words. *Just* as she finished speaking, and *just* as I was about to yell ahead to the kids not to cross Central Park West without us, they turned around and began singing loudly, "For they are jolly good sitters, for they are jolly good sitters, for they are jolly good sit-*ters*, which nobody can deny." (Except for Grace, who sang, "For they are jelly good sitters, which nobody can peny.")

I'm sure my face turned red. Kristy's did. And so did Claudia's, Mary Anne's and Dawn's. A bunch of people were nearby, watching and smiling. At first I wanted to hurry the kids across the street and home, away from our audience. Then I thought, How come everything embarrasses me so much? How come *this* embarrasses me? It's cute. The kids are doing this because they like us and they had a good time today.

"Thanks, you guys!" I called, running to catch up with the kids.

"Yeah, thanks!" cried my friends.

And the fifteen of us formed our Madeline lines again and crossed the street, tired and happy. We took a left and hup-two'd down the sidewalk. We turned onto my street and passed Judy.

Blair decided to try again. "Hup, two!" he said to Judy.

"Hup, two!" she replied. Then she noticed me and added, "Hello, Missy."

Blair grinned.

We marched to our building, past James and Isaac and Lloyd, into the elevator, and rose up and up. Our adventure was over.

CHAPTER 13

Dear Logan,

As Claudia would say, "Oh, my lord!" You will not believe what we did last night. We had the most glamorous, exciting Saturday night in the history of the universe. We went to a Broadway play. We sat right in the middle of the theater, up close. And we ate dinner out — just the five of us, plus Stacey's friend Laine. And we RODE IN A LIMO. (Limo is short for limousine.) We really did. This is the truth. Uh-oh, I've run out of room, so I'll have to tell you the rest when we get back.

Love,
Mary Anne

After what happened between Laine and Claudia the night before, I would never have believed that we'd spend Saturday evening with Laine. But we did. And what an evening it was. Did we ever have fun! You know one reason I had so much fun? Because I pretended I was a tourist, not a native New Yorker. I saw everything through new eyes. But before I go any further, let me tell you how the evening came about, and how our baby-sitting adventure ended.

When we reached my apartment, we found it full of people. All the parents were there, waiting for their kids. The meeting had ended earlier, and everyone was talking about the homelessness problem. They stopped when we came in, though, and for a few moments, there was pandemonium.

Grace literally threw herself at her mother. The Deluca kids chattered away nonstop. Leslie announced, "I almost threw up, but didn't."

Mrs. Reames looked horrified. "Did you eat something with wheat in it?" she cried. She was talking to Leslie but looking at me — accusingly.

"No, no," I said hurriedly. "A little too much ice cream, I think. On top of too much excitement."

Henry chose that moment to say to his father, "I got lost! But then I got found."

Mary Anne told Mr. Walker what had happened in the museum.

For the most part, the kids were excited and enthusiastic, so their parents were pleased. When everyone left, Mom and Dad and my friends and I collapsed in the living room. My parents seemed as tired as we did.

"The meeting was *very* long," said Mom.

"But productive," added Dad. "We made a lot of headway. We came up with some plans that should start to help Judy and the other homeless people around here. For one thing, we're going to open a soup kitchen."

"One of the churches is going to help us, too," Mom was saying when the phone rang.

I answered it in the kitchen. "Hello?"

"Hi, it's me." Laine.

"Hi!" I replied. I know Laine had said she would call, but considering how badly the party had gone, I was a little surprised to hear from her.

"How was the baby-sitting?" she asked.

I told her about our adventure.

Then Laine went on, "Well, guess what. You won't believe this." She paused dramatically. "I'm not sure whether to tell you about this, but, well, Dad got free tickets — house seats, excellent ones — to *Starlight Express*. They're for tonight.

116

He and Mom don't want to go, so he offered them to me. This may be a bad idea, but would you and your friends like to go to the play? He could get six seats, all together. And he'd order us the limo. I don't know about Claudia, but I feel awful about last night, and I'd kind of like to start over."

I should explain a few things here. One, Laine's father is a big-time producer of Broadway plays. That's how the Cummingses got enough money to move into the Dakota, and that's why Laine's father is always being given tickets to things. Two, the tickets he's given are usually for "house seats," which are also in really prime locations. Like about six rows back (not up in some balcony that's two miles away from the stage), and smack in the middle of the theater. Three, the Cummingses are forever hiring this limo to take them places. They don't own a car (owning a car is a real pain in New York), but instead of taking cabs, they get this lo-o-o-ong limo. It's called a stretch limo and can seat about a million people and has a bar and a TV inside. When the chauffeur beeps the horn, it plays the first two lines from "Home on the Range."

I, of course, was completely bowled over by Laine's invitation. Free tickets? Six of them? The *limo*? But I knew I had to check with my parents and my friends. I told Laine I'd call her back. Then, after getting permission from Mom and Dad to go to the play, I gathered my friends in my bedroom.

"So what do you think?" I asked when I'd explained the situation. I watched their eyes grow wider and wider, so I knew they were excited. Possibly, Mary Anne had become catatonic. She seemed unable to move or speak.

Still, I kept remembering Laine calling Claudia a jerk, and Claudia calling Laine a stuck-up snob, and everybody accusing each other of things.

"Laine says she wants to start over, to try again," I added.

Claudia cleared her throat. "We-ell," she said slowly. "If Laine wants to try again, then so do I. And I promise I'll really give her a chance."

"Ya-hoo!" Kristy shouted, jumping to her feet.

"Broadway . . . wow," Mary Anne managed to say.

Dawn looked at Claudia. "Oh, my lord," she said, and giggled.

Then I called Laine back. We agreed to meet for dinner at this little restaurant that's between our apartments. After dinner, the limo would take us downtown to the play. Later, it would bring us home.

Mary Anne immediately became hysterical about clothing. This time I was able to say, "You guys, wear the fanciest outfits you brought."

In all honesty, people don't necessarily get dressed up for the theater anymore. You see everything from blue jeans to fur coats there. (Often, you see jeans and a fur coat on *the same person.*) But since my friends and I were going to be arriving and leaving in a limo, I decided it would be fun to get very dressed up.

This presented a problem for Kristy, but she borrowed a dress from Mary Anne, some accessories from Dawn and Claudia, and a pair of shoes from me. She was all set. When the five of us left the bedroom and entered the living room, my parents made a big fuss over us.

"Let me just take your picture," said Mom. (She took twelve.)

"Have a great evening," my father added. He slipped me some money. "Now if *any*thing goes wrong, call us. Do you have change?" (I nodded.) "I don't even want you taking a cab by yourselves late at night. So if something happens with the limo, try to find a nice, well-lit coffee shop and call from there. Don't stand around on the street."

"We could hang around in the theater," I said

hopefully, thinking of the stars we might see there. "I could call from the lobby."

Dad barely heard me. He had a lot more instructions to give out. So did Mom. They were worried about letting us loose for the evening. Mom was so worried, that as we left the apartment she said, "Have fun and be very, VERY careful."

I was worried about other things. Namely, how everyone would get along that night. As we walked to the restaurant, my heart began to pound.

But the thought of the free tickets and the limo must have mellowed my friends out. When we reached the restaurant, Laine was already there and she and Claudia just smiled sheepishly at each other.

A waiter seated us at a large round table, and we ordered our food. Nobody did any apologizing. (It didn't seem necessary.) But nobody did any sniping, either.

Laine told us about the play we were going to see. "It's the story of a train race. My father said the set is really amazing. The costumes, too. And every actor and actress is on roller skates."

"You're kidding!" exclaimed Claudia. "That's awesome."

Somehow, we started talking about places we'd visited. Laine was going to California over Christmas and had never been there before. So Dawn told her about California. Then Laine told us about a trip to Japan she'd been on. Claudia was fascinated.

I couldn't believe it when I looked at my watch and saw that the time was 7:35. "We better get going!" I cried. "The show starts at eight."

"Yeah, the limo must be here," added Laine.

It was. It was right in front of the restaurant. We climbed inside, feeling like celebrities and hoping someone would see us. Then we turned on the TV for a few seconds (just so Kristy would be able to tell people that she'd actually watched TV in a limousine), examined the bar, and settled back to watch the streets slip by as we zipped downtown to the Gershwin Theatre.

We were ushered to our seats. The magnificent set spread before us. No curtain was hiding it, so the audience could get a good look at the hills and roads and passages that snaked around the stage for the roller skaters.

At 8:05 the play began. We were in awe. The cast roared through the set at top speed, taking curves practically on the edges of their wheels. Sometimes they looked like they were going to fly right off the stage and into the audience. The story seemed like an old one (will the underdog beat out the mean new guy in the race?), but there was so much action that we were on the edges of our seats from the beginning until the end.

When it was over, Mary Anne sighed with pleasure. "A Broadway play. A limo. I've died and gone to heaven."

We left the theater and climbed back in the limousine. We were tired, but we just talked and talked all the way home. Claudia and Laine began teasing me.

"Once Stacey left her lunch on the radiator," said Laine, "and it smelled up the whole classroom. That was in fourth grade."

"Once she had to baby-sit for some snob kids and she used this weird kind of psychology," said Claudia. "She tamed the kids all right, but they thought she was nuts."

We laughed. And since we were getting along so well, I said, "Laine? You want to spend the night? You could make up for last night."

Laine looked thoughtful. "I do want to," she answered, "but I think you guys need time to visit alone. I mean, without me. We had fun this evening — and, Claud, I'm really happy I got to know the *real* you — but now I should probably go home."

She was right. I was glad Laine felt she could be so honest with us. The evening, I decided, had been perfect. Not only had it been fun, but now that the members of the Baby-sitters Club had relaxed and gotten used to traveling together and being in New York, they'd been able to feel comfortable with Laine.

The limo cruised up the West Side, dropped my friends and me off in front of my building, and then headed for the Dakota with Laine.

But before Claudia climbed out of the car, she and Laine exchanged phone numbers and addresses.

CHAPTER 14

Dear Shannon,

   Hi! How's our associate club member? Have you had any interesting baby-sitting jobs this weekend? Wait till you hear about the one we had. It involved ten children and Central Park, but I'll tell you more the next time I see you. After our sitting job, we went out to dinner, and rode to a Broadway play in a LIMOUSINE. Then we tried to have a (fake) club meeting, for old times' sake. I wish you had known Stacey better. I think the *two of you would have been friends.*

See you soon!
Kristy

Our club meeting was really fun (a lot more fun than the uncomfortable one we'd held that morning), but it wasn't an actual meeting at all. We were just fooling around. It really was "fake," as Kristy had written to Shannon Kilbourne. (By the way, in case you're wondering, an associate club member is someone who doesn't come to meetings, but whom my friends can call on if they're offered a job they're too busy to take. Sort of a backup. They have two associate members. Shannon is one. Guess who the other is? Logan, Mary Anne's boyfriend!)

When Dawn, Claudia, Kristy, Mary Anne, and I entered my apartment, Mom and Dad were waiting up for us (of course). They looked only a little worried, and as soon as they saw that we were in one piece and heard that we'd had a good time, they went to bed.

My friends and I looked at each other. Great! The night was ours. Remember how tired we'd been after· our afternoon of sitting? And how tired we'd been when we climbed into the limo to come home? Well, suddenly we weren't tired anymore. We got our second winds.

"Everybody, change into your nightgowns and come to my room," I said.

"Oh, good," said Kristy. "Let's have a meeting of the Baby-sitters Club."

Fifteen minutes later, Claudia and I were lying across my bed on our stomachs, Mary Anne and Dawn were sitting cross-legged on the floor, and Kristy was settled in my armchair.

"This meeting of the Baby-sitters Club," said Kristy, "will now come to order." Usually Kristy speaks fairly loudly, but since Mom and Dad were nearby, trying to sleep, she kept her voice down. "Any official business?" she asked.

"No," we replied.

"Any problems with the club notebook or record book?"

"No."

"They're not *here*," Claudia added.

"Just play along," I whispered, nudging her.

"Anybody had any sitting jobs she needs to talk about?"

Well, now this was getting out of hand. It was silly. No one was really paying attention to

Kristy. Dawn and Mary Anne were trying on my sparkly silver nail polish. Claudia was looking longingly at a movie magazine on my desk.

Kristy sensed that she did not have control of the "meeting."

I spoke up. "This doesn't have much to do with baby-sitting, Kristy, but how are things going at Watson's? How are Karen and Andrew?"

"Oh, they're great!" said Kristy. (She loves to talk about her little stepsister and stepbrother. I knew I could get her off the subject of baby-sitting. I just knew it.) "And I'll tell you something," she went on. "I hardly think of the house as 'Watson's' anymore. It's just 'ours.' All of ours. Mom's, Watson's, Charlie's, Sam's, David Michael's, Andrew's, Karen's, mine, and even Shannon's and Boo-Boo's." (Shannon is David Michael's puppy, and Boo-Boo is Watson's cat. Shannon is named for Shannon Kilbourne, the associate club member. It's a long story.)

"That's great," I said. "So you feel like you're fitting in? I mean, in the neighborhood?"

"I'm getting there," Kristy replied.

"How about you, Dawn?" I wanted to know.

"How about me?" Dawn repeated vaguely. She had painted her fingernails and was now putting a tiny dot of silver polish in the center of each toenail. She looked up. "Oh, you mean fitting in in Stoneybrook?"

I nodded.

"I hardly even think about it anymore," she replied. "Getting used to the Jeff thing is much harder."

"The Jeff thing?"

Silence. Four heads turned toward me.

"Don't you know?" asked Claudia, aghast. "I was sure I told you."

"Know what? I don't remember you telling me anything. Tell me now!"

My friends glanced at Dawn, who had finished dotting her toenails.

Dawn handed the bottle of polish to Mary Anne, and looked quite uncomfortable. At last she said, "My brother moved back to my dad."

"He moved to California?" I cried. Then I clapped my hand over my mouth, realizing how loudly I'd spoken. "I knew there were problems," I went on quietly. "I guess I even knew your mom was considering letting him go back, but I didn't know it had actually happened. Oh, Dawn, I'm really sorry."

I don't know how close Dawn and her younger brother are, but being an only child I sometimes fantasize about having a brother or sister. It seems like the most wonderful thing in the world. So losing a brother or sister seemed like the most horrible thing in the world.

Dawn's eyes filled with tears. She blinked them away. Then she said, "Well, it's no wonder you didn't know. Remember what was going on at the same time Jeff was getting ready to leave?"

Claudia, Mary Anne, and Kristy burst out laughing.

"The Little Miss Stoneybrook Pageant!" Claudia cried. "What a mess!"

"Tell me more about it," I said eagerly, wishing I'd still been in Stoneybrook then. "I only heard bits and pieces."

"It started with me," said Dawn, who seemed to have recovered. "It was this pageant for five- to eight-year-old girls, and Claire and Margo Pike were dying to be in it, so their mother gave me the job of preparing them to enter. Each girl had to have a talent. You know what Margo's was? Peeling a banana with her feet and reciting *The House That Jack Built*."

Every single one of us became hysterical. We grabbed pillows and stuffed them over our faces to muffle our laughter.

But Dawn was on a roll. "And you know what Claire's talent was?" she went on. "She sang, *I'm Popeye the sailor man. I live in a garbage can. I eat all the wor-orms and spit out the ger-erms. I'm Popeye the sailor man."*

We could barely contain ourselves.

"I'm going to wet my pants!" exclaimed Claudia who was laughing so hard she was crying. She dashed for the bathroom.

When Claudia returned, Dawn said in a whisper, "You guys, I have just had the *best* idea. Let's goof-call Jeff in California. It's only eight-thirty out there."

"Okay," I agreed, "but just one call. It's expensive. What should we say?"

"Let's see if he falls for the oldest goof-call in telephone history," suggested Mary Anne. "Oh, please, Dawn, can I call him?"

"Sure," replied Dawn. She gave Mary Anne her father's phone number.

Mary Anne dialed it. "It's ringing," she told us. Pause. Then she cupped her hand over the receiver. "*Jeff* answered!" she whispered loudly. She removed her hand. "Hello?" she said. "Is your refrigerator running?"

"Yeah, I think so," Jeff replied.

"Then you better go catch it!" cried Mary Anne gleefully, and hung up.

Further hysteria. I laughed until I rolled off the bed. Then an awful thought occurred to me.

"Dawn!" I said. "What if Jeff thought that was you and he calls your house? *Now?* He'll wake up your mom."

After a moment of horrified silence we started laughing again. We just couldn't help it.

"I bet," said Mary Anne, "that if he called *my* house now, he'd get a busy signal. You know why?"

"Because your father has a girlfriend and spends hours talking on the phone with her?" I teased.

"*No.* Because Tigger knows how to take the phone off the hook and he does it all the time."

"You're kidding!" I cried. "Tigger's only a kitten."

"It's true!" said Dawn. "I've seen him do it. It's the phone on Mr. Spier's desk. He bats the receiver until it falls off."

At this point, I was afraid my parents were going to come in and tell us to stop being so noisy (it was impossible to calm down), so I told my friends we had to move into the living room.

"Good," said Claudia as we tiptoed down the hall. "I'm hungry and the living room is closer to the kitchen. Got any junk food?"

"Party leftovers," I told her.

We raided the refrigerator. Then we sat around the living room eating heroes and potato chips and pretzels. (Well, not me. I just had a diet soda. I have to be extremely careful about my food intake because of my diabetes. And Dawn had only pretzels and the tomatoes from one of the heros, since she won't touch the meat inside.)

"Boy," said Kristy after she swallowed a mouthful of potato chips. "I wish we'd had as much fun at the party last night as we're having now."

"I guess you guys were too nervous," I said. "Maybe a party your first day here wasn't such a good idea."

"I don't know why I was so nervous," spoke up Claudia. "Maybe I was trying too hard to fit in. I'm sorry about Coby, Kristy."

"That's okay," Kristy replied. "I overreacted. Anyway, Coby has my phone number and address and I have his. I bet we'll be in touch soon." Kristy blushed, but I knew she was pleased with the idea of writing or talking to . . . a boy!

"As long as we're apologizing," said Mary Anne, "I'm sorry I've been such a pain. I mean about New York. It's just that it's such a glamorous place."

"Well, *I'm* sorry I've been such a scaredy-cat," said Dawn. "New York always seemed like such a frightening place."

"I'm sorry I haven't been very understanding," I added.

And Kristy said, "And I'm sorry I have such a big mouth."

With that, we started giggling again. We talked and giggled until Mom really did have to get up and tell us to be quiet. Then we went to bed.

CHAPTER 15

Dear Jessi,

Writing this postcard is ridiculous, because we're on the train coming home now. It's a New York postcard and I'll be mailing it in Stoneybrook! Oh, well. Today was great because the five of us were just being ourselves so we were having a blast. It was sad Because we had to say good-bye to Stacey. Anyway, this is

Guess what just happened? Kristy is asleep next to me and her head keeps falling on my arm! I better end here. Claudia wants to go to the snack car for M&M's and

Love, Dawn

It was our last day together and guess how we spent half the morning? Sleeping! We were exhausted. We hadn't fallen asleep until about one o'clock the night before. I hated to waste time sleeping, but it felt so nice to keep stretching my legs out in bed and rolling over for "just five more minutes." (Each five minutes lasted at least fifteen minutes, and I must have done that eight times.)

Anyway, when my clock read 10:08, I finally yawned and stretched and struggled to sit up. Then I wandered into the living room to see what was going on. I found a note from my parents saying they'd gone to church and then planned to take a walk. I felt kind of sorry for them. With the club members asleep in the living room and den, there was no place my parents could go except the kitchen or their bedroom — or outside.

I hated to wake everyone up, but it had to be done. My friends' train was leaving at two-thirty that afternoon, and we didn't want to sleep away our last few hours. I began making kitchen noises. I put up a kettle of water for tea, got out plates and knives, and then opened the refrigerator, hoping to find what I usually find there on Sunday morning — lox and cream cheese. In a paper bag in the bread drawer were fresh bagels. Goody!

"Oh, you guys!" I called. "Breakfast time!"

I heard rumblings and muffled, sleepy sounds from the other rooms, but nothing else.

I put the bagels on a platter, the lox on a plate, and the cream cheese on another plate. A breakfast assembly line was now ready — if anyone would get up.

"Yoo-hoo!" I called.

"*Yoo*-hoo?" replied Kristy. "You sound like my grandmother."

"Come *on*. Get *up*. I've got a great breakfast for you. Even you will like it, Dawn." We had whole-wheat bagels as well as regular ones, so Dawn wouldn't have to poison her body with white bread.

I heard thumps, and rustlings, and soon my bleary-eyed friends had found their way into the kitchen.

Kristy's eyes bugged out at the plate of bright orange lox. "*What* is *that?*" she asked, pointing.

"Lox," I replied.

"I'm hoping," said Kristy, "that lox isn't what it looks like, which is fish."

"It is fish," I told her. "Salmon."

"*Raw?*"

"Smoked."

"Is it like sushi?" asked Mary Anne warily.

"No, it's cooked," I said. "It just looks raw."

"I'll try it," said Dawn. She paused. "How do you eat it?"

"Like this," I answered. "I'll fix you a breakfast you won't forget."

"I bet," muttered Kristy.

I sliced a bagel in half, toasted the halves in the toaster, slathered them with cream cheese, placed some lox on top, arranged the bagel halves on a plate, and presented the plate to Dawn.

She took a bite. "This," she said, closing her eyes, "is heaven. Food heaven."

"I now pronounce you a true New Yorker," I said.

"You mean I won't be a true New Yorker until I eat smoked orange fish?" asked Mary Anne.

"That's right."

"Oh, lord," said Claudia.

Well, in the end, all my friends wanted to be true New Yorkers, so they ate the lox and bagels. Even Kristy. Then we got dressed (we wore our Hard Rock Cafe T-shirts), and we sat around and read the *New York Times*, which Mom and Dad brought home with them when they finally returned.

"A New York City Sunday morning tradition," I said.

"Really?" asked Mary Anne. She looked quite pleased with herself. Then she glanced at her watch and her expression changed to utter sadness.

"What's wrong?" asked Dawn.

"It's noon."

"Oh, wow. In less than two hours we'll have to leave for the train station," I said.

At that moment the doorbell rang.

Good. A diversion. I ran for it.

"Who's there?" I called.

"It's Mrs. Walker."

I opened the door. There stood Mrs. Walker with Henry and Grace.

"Hi!" I said.

"Hi," answered Mrs. Walker.

Henry and Grace scooted behind their mother and peeped around at me, but they were smiling.

"Come on in," I told them.

They did. Henry and Grace each held out a piece of drawing paper.

"These are for you . . . and your friends," said Henry.

"Hey, you guys, come here!" I called.

Kristy, Dawn, Mary Anne, and Claudia joined us in the hallway.

"This was the kids' idea," said Mrs. Walker. "They were up early, drawing pictures, and they said they wanted you to have these. They had a great time yesterday."

"Thanks!" said my friends and I.

Henry's picture was identifiable as a dinosaur. (A stegosaurus, he informed us.) Grace's was a blue circle with some squiggly pink and green lines around it. She said it was Central Park.

After the Walkers left, my friends decided that they wanted to say good-bye to the other kids we had sat for, so we did just that, only this time we started with the apartment on the lowest floor and worked our way up. Dawn rode the elevator like she'd been doing it all her life. Mary Anne didn't quote one fact about New York, Kristy didn't make a single snide remark, and Claudia mentioned that she was going to write a letter to Laine when she got home.

So my friends said their good-byes to Dennis and Sean, to Carlos, Blair, and Cissy, and to Natalie and Peggie. As we left the Upchurches' apartment and headed for the elevator, Kristy stopped in her tracks.

"You know something," she said, "I don't *want* to go say good-bye to Leslie Reames. We'll probably get stuck in that penthouse listening to a lecture on wheat allergies . . . or what would happen to Leslie if she ate goat cheese."

We laughed.

"Well, we have to go," I said. "You can't say good-bye to all the kids except Leslie."

Reluctantly, we rode to the penthouse. But Martha was the only one there. Hooray! Unfortunately, now my friends had to pack their things. It was time for them to get ready to leave.

The packing was done silently. We weren't mad, just sad.

We lugged Claudia's boxcar into the living room.

My friends said good-bye to Mom and Dad.

Then my father gave me some money for a taxi, and we left the apartment.

"Thanks for everything!" said my friends.

"Come back soon," my father replied.

"We loved having you," added Mom.

Claudia looked at me mischievously and whispered, "Have fun and be careful."

"Have fun and be careful!" Mom called, just as the elevator arrived.

We zoomed to the ground floor.

"Have a good day!" said Isaac as we trooped by.

I hailed a cab. The driver put Claudia's boxcar in the trunk. My friends and I squeezed their duffels and knapsacks and souvenirs into the taxi.

The ride to Grand Central was pretty quiet.

We weren't sure what to say to each other. But as soon as we entered the train station we all began talking at once.

"What a weekend!" exclaimed Mary Anne.

"Oh, my lord, it's been awesome!" said Claud.

"I'm glad we got to meet Laine," said Dawn.

"This building is the hottest place I've ever been in," complained Kristy.

"Worse than Bloomingdale's?" I asked her.

"Hmm. That's a close one to call."

Unfortunately, my friends' train was announced then. In a split second, every one of us burst into tears, even Kristy.

We hugged and cried and said how much we would miss each other and made all sorts of promises about writing and phoning and visiting.

Then I walked the members of the Stoneybrook branch of the Baby-sitters Club to their track.

"Good-bye," said my friends together.

"Good-bye," I replied. "Have fun and be careful!"

About the Author

Ann M. Martin's The Baby-sitters Club has sold over 190 million copies and inspired a generation of young readers. Her novels include the Newbery Honor Book *A Corner of the Universe*, *A Dog's Life*, and the Main Street series. She lives in upstate New York.

Keep reading for a sneak peek at the next book
from The Baby-sitters Club!

Claudia and the Bad Joke

When dinner was over, Mom and Dad and Janine cleared the table and began cleaning the kitchen. Mimi and I went into the living room to do my homework. It's sort of a family rule that some-body has to give me a hand with my homework each night. This is because my grades used to be so bad. My homework was always a mess, and I didn't know how to study for tests or quizzes.

The best homework nights are the ones on which Mimi helps me. The worst are the ones on which Janine helps me. I wish I didn't have to have any help at all, but my parents told me I couldn't stay in the Baby-sitters Club unless I kept my grades up.

"All right," Mimi began, "what are your assign — assign — what is homework?"

"One page of math problems, read this chapter in my science book, and answer these questions for English," I told her.

Mimi nodded. "Where to start?"

"English," I said promptly. I don't love English, but I *hate* math and science.

"Why not get bad work done first, then do English?" suggested Mimi.

I screwed up my face. "Okay," I agreed.

We began with the math. I don't know what it is about numbers. They just don't make sense to me. Stacey once said that she can "read" numbers the way she can read words. She understands them. She can look at a problem for a few moments, and suddenly she has the answer, without doing any figuring or writing. She calculates things in her head as if her brain were a computer.

Not me. Oh, no. I sit and figure, and half the

time I'm figuring wrong. Adding when I should be multiplying, subtracting four from ten and getting seven. What a mess!

Mimi and I plodded through my work. Mimi is *so* patient. She never raises her voice or gets aggravated.

"Now," she said, when I had finished my math and science, "where are English plobrems, my Claudia?"

I knew she had meant to say "problems." "They're just some questions," I told her, "and they're right here."

In English class this year we're reading the Newbery Award–winning books. We've already read several. Now we're reading *Roll of Thunder, Hear My Cry*. I didn't think I would like it, but really, it isn't bad.

Mimi looked at the list of questions and read the first one. "In what — in what ways is main — is *the* main character in *Roll of*, um, *Thunder, Hear My Cry* simi — similar to main — to *the* main character in *A Wrinkle in Time*?"

"Oh, lord," I replied, "They couldn't be more different! I hate questions like that."

"Think, my Claudia. Is *any*thing the same about them?"

"They're both girls," I said.

If Janine had been helping me, she probably would have thrown down her pencil in disgust at that answer, but Mimi just said, "That a good start. What else?"

We worked and worked. The more we talked, the more answers I found. When we were finally done, I kissed Mimi, thanked her, and escaped to my room.

Ah, art. I looked at the half-finished pastel drawing on my easel. I just stood in front of it for several minutes, thinking. After awhile, I opened my box of pastels and slowly set to work. When I'm in the middle of a good project, especially a painting or a drawing, I can forget about everything else. Which is what I did. And which may explain why I jumped a mile when the phone rang.

"Hello?" I said.

"Hi, Claudia. It's Ashley."

Ashley Wyeth is a new friend of mine. We have a funny relationship. It seems like we're always mad at each other. We're forever fighting, then making up. But Ashley is the only person who truly understands my love of art. She's an artist herself — the most talented person our age I know. Before she moved to Stoneybrook, she lived in Chicago and went to this really great art school there. And *she* thinks *I'm* talented! Ashley can be a pain in the neck, though, because she's always bugging me to quit baby-sitting and spend more time on my art.

So when Ashley called, I braced myself for a lecture, but all she wanted was our English assignment. I read her the questions and then hung up. As soon as I did, the phone rang again.

"Hello?"

At first there was just silence at the other end of the phone. Then an odd-sounding voice said, "Do you have Prince Albert in a can?"

"Huh?" I replied. "Prince Albert?"

"Oh, never mind." The voice suddenly sounded disgusted and the caller hung up.

I looked at the receiver as if it could explain to me what had just happened. A goof call gone wrong, I decided as I hung up. The caller was probably someone who'd been at the film festival. Practical-joke season had begun — and I, for one, did not like it.

Want more baby-sitting?

And many more!

Don't miss any of the books in the Baby-sitters Club series by Ann M. Martin—available as ebooks

DON'T MISS THE BABY-SITTERS LITTLE SISTER GRAPHIC NOVELS!

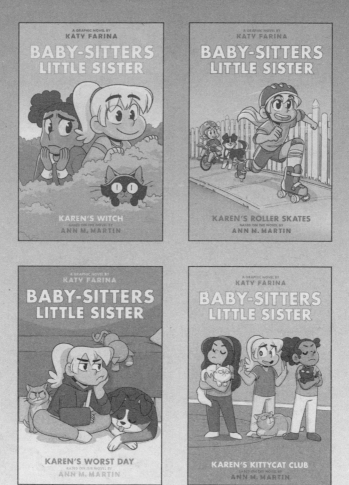

It's fun to be a

LITTLE SISTER®

Read more of Karen's adventures!

#1 Karen's Witch   #2 Karen's Roller Skates

#3 Karen's Worst Day   #4 Karen's Kittycat Club